James Stirling

As Regards Protoplasm

Anatiposi

James Stirling

As Regards Protoplasm

Reprint of the original, first published in 1872.

1st Edition 2023 | ISBN: 978-3-38216-626-7

Anatiposi Verlag is an imprint of Outlook Verlagsgesellschaft mbH.

Verlag (Publisher): Outlook Verlag GmbH, Zeilweg 44, 60439 Frankfurt, Deutschland
Vertretungsberechtigt (Authorized to represent): E. Roepke, Zeilweg 44, 60439 Frankfurt, Deutschland
Druck (Print): Books on Demand GmbH, In de Tarpen 42, 22848 Norderstedt, Deutschland

AS REGARDS PROTOPLASM.

BY

JAMES HUTCHISON STIRLING,

F.R.C.S., AND LL.D., EDIN.

New and Improved Edition,

COMPLETED BY ADDITION OF

PART II.,

IN REFERENCE TO MR HUXLEY'S *SECOND ISSUE,*

AND OF

PREFACE,

IN REPLY TO MR HUXLEY IN " *YEAST.*"

LONDON: LONGMANS, GREEN, & CO.

1872.

COLSTON & SON, LAW AND GENERAL PRINTERS, EDINBURGH.

PREFACE.

————

WHEN this Essay was first published, the following was the prefatory note (October 1869):—

" The substance of the greater part of this paper, which has been in the present form for some time, was delivered, as a lecture, at a Conversazione of the Royal College of Physicians of Edinburgh, in the Hall of the College, on the evening of Friday, the 30th of April last.

It will be found to support itself, so far as the facts are concerned, on the most recent German physiological literature, as represented by Rindfleisch, Kühne, and especially Stricker, with which last, for the production of his 'Handbuch,' there is associated every great histological name in Germany."

I may now state, without any more particular reference to the motives, whether general or special, which gave rise to it, that this essay of mine had but one thing to do,—to protest, namely, against the thoughtless extinction of certain essential *differences* in a supposed *common identity*. I may illustrate this by a remark in a letter to me on the subject by the late lamented Professor Ueberweg, which (the letter itself is dated Jan. 16, 1870) is as follows:—" As I am neither a physiologist nor a zoologist, I cannot be expected to follow your argument into its details, but I am vividly interested by its logical or dialectical leading thought—the contention, namely, for the right of the logical category of Difference, as against that of Identity one-sidedly accentuated, as it seems, by Huxley." My reply to this was, " that he (Ueberweg) had hit the mark—that I had been simply laughing all through, and holding up to the category of identity, the *equally authentic* category of difference —but that it had taken a German to find me out."

In the same letter, Ueberweg proceeded to say that the question, in the first place, therefore, was evidently a *logical* one. Now this, doubtless, is true; but this, nevertheless, is not enough. If the question involves at bottom logical issues, it has been really addressed by Mr Huxley to physiological ones; and it is only in the interest of scientific accuracy to point out that the inference to a physiological identity has been attempted to be made good by Mr Huxley, solely through means of an unwarrantable trampling out of (perhaps, for the moment, involuntary blindness to) the most essential physiological differences. For example, if you *identify* all life in protoplasm, the counter-reminder is only fair that you must equally *differentiate* all life in protoplasm*s*; for of no one living thing, and of the organs of no one living thing, is the protoplasm interchangeable with that of another; and this involves, instead of Mr Huxley's universal *identity* in power, in form, and in substance, infinite *difference* in all these respects.

In the statement of this difference—which is really a veritable scientific interest—I was led into a variety of expositions, and, among these, into an historical one. So far, now, as it was *history* that was concerned in this, I could not, of course, in one way, take any credit to myself; still it was precisely here that, in another way, I did think I might take some little credit to myself. If in the course of the essay, indeed, there was anything else that seemed to me similarly situated, it was the summaries—the summaries of Mr Huxley's views, namely, with which I always prefaced my criticism of these. I confess that I thought them *exact*—short, that is, to the shortest, but full to the fullest, and certainly fair to the fairest, if not also clear to the clearest. It has pleased Mr Huxley, however, rudely to shock my not immoderate complacency in both respects. Neither history nor summaries, it seems, can he regard with satisfaction. That is, it was alone for what was not mine in the whole essay that I allowed myself to take any credit *as* mine, and this Mr Huxley denies me. In the reply, namely, to which, after two years' interval, he has at length brought himself, it has pleased Mr Huxley—in those few sour-humoured words of his in the *Contemporary Review* for December 1871—to call the history a "travesty," and (by implication) the summaries "utter misrepresentations." That Mr Huxley, fairly looking at either history or summaries, should yet feel himself free to speak so, throws me back—I confess it—on thoughts of *him*.

If, as I say, the summaries could not, as wholly referring to the matter of another, be called my own, so neither could the history be called my own, and for a like reason. Nevertheless, as I also say, I had such consciousness of *honest work* in either respect, that I could not help allowing myself a certain satisfaction in both. The grounds, more especially for this as regards the history—the summaries I dismiss for the present—lay as well in the *pains* that still throbbed before consciousness, as in the fact that the narrative involved was known to me to be then only for the first time presented in English.* I fancied, indeed, that Mr Huxley himself would applaud here, for I believed him partial to a scientific historiette. Had I but known that he had *in petto* a *rival* history! I confess I had no anticipations of this: and, as to that indeed, perhaps he had it not *in petto*. Perhaps Mr Huxley has only benevolently got it up since—*for my correction—by example of him?* There at least it is—my historiette is a "travesty," it seems, and Mr Huxley, in the pages of the *Contemporary Review*, replaces it by *his*. Loudly! Ay, Mr Huxley, I venture to say, is not less loud here than the legitimate blind beggar whom Mr Horne represents to abuse the interloping one thus:—

> " I am the genuine blind man,
>   That villain seeks to grind one,
>   And poach one's field ;
>   But I'll not yield,—
>   What ! leave old rights behind one !
>
> " *I* am the real blind man,
>   The genuine real blind man !
>   As for that thief
>   With eyes, may grief
>   Consume him !   *I* am the blind man !"

But it will be only fair to Mr Huxley that the readers of the present essay should see his objections to it in his own words. The yeast-organism affording him an exceedingly eligible starting-ground for his lively representative ways, Mr Huxley begins with it, and is thereby enabled to give a little, not unwelcome, additional show of bulk to—after all—the somewhat *scanty* historical forces he has only desperately driven together. With these skilful preliminary dispositions, the attack itself—and in its entirety—is this :—

" Dr Stirling, for example, made my essay the subject of a

---

* By way of *indirect* testimony here, let me refer to an eminent physiological Professor who, on a late occasion, speaking of protoplasm, before the British Association, displayed this severe impartiality between us that, while he gave *my* account of protoplasm, it was Mr Huxley alone he *named !*

special critical lecture, which I have read with much interest,
though, I confess, the meaning of much of it remains as dark to
me as does the ' Secret of Hegel,' after Dr Stirling's elaborate
revelation of it.   Dr Stirling's method of dealing with the subject is peculiar.   ' Protoplasm ' is a question of history, so far as
it is a name ; of fact, so far as it is a thing.   Dr Stirling has
not taken the trouble to refer to the original authorities for his
history, which is consequently a travesty ; and, still less, has he
concerned himself with looking at the facts, but contents himself with taking them also at second hand.   A most amusing
example of this fashion of dealing with scientific statements is
furnished by Dr Stirling's remarks upon my account of the
protoplasm of the nettle hair.   That account was drawn up
from careful and often-repeated observation of the facts.   Dr
Stirling thinks he is offering a valid criticism, when he says that
my valued friend, Professor Stricker, gives a somewhat different
statement about protoplasm.   But why in the world did not
this distinguished Hegelian look at a nettle hair for himself,
before venturing to speak about the matter at all?   Why trouble
himself about what either Stricker or I say, when any tyro can
see the facts for himself, if he is provided with those not rare
articles—a nettle and a microscope?   But I suppose this would
have been 'Aufklärung'—a recurrence to the base common-sense
philosophy of the eighteenth century, which liked to see before
it believed, and to understand before it criticised.   Dr Stirling
winds up his paper with the following paragraph :—' In short,
the whole position of Mr Huxley, (1) that all organisms consist
alike of the same life-matter, (2) which life-matter is, for its
part, due only to chemistry, must be pronounced untenable—
nor less untenable (3) the materialism he would found on it.'

" The paragraph contains three distinct assertions concerning
my views, and just the same number of utter misrepresentations of them.   That which I have numbered (1) turns on the
ambiguity of the word ' same,' for a discussion of which I
would refer Dr Stirling to a great hero of ' Aufklärung,' Archbishop Whately; statement number (2) is, in my judgment,
absurd; and certainly I have never said anything resembling
it; while, as to number (3), one great object of my essay was
to show that what is called ' materialism ' has no sound philosophical basis !"

Now this, so far as it is anything, is, as one sees, clever; but it is not an answer : it is only *business*. " My flock will expect a word from me, and will probably not be the worse of one: it will be, so far, a satisfaction to them, and convenient in use, perhaps !"

Be the nature of the cleverity what it may, then, one must pity the necessity of the shift; and, but for Mr Huxley's authority with the public—an authority quite just in its place, doubtless—the record, so far as I am concerned, might very well close here. That authority considered, however, perhaps it would be only duly respectful to the public—and even to Mr Huxley himself—that I should examine his observations in reply to my essay *seriatim* and at full. This, then, I shall now do.

To begin at the end, and travel *gradually* upwards, I must avow that it is certainly clever to take the three short clauses of the short concluding sentence of my essay as together representative of the whole, and so, in destroying them, destroy it ! There is management in this—especially in view of Dr Beale's quotation of the sentence; but the question remains—has Mr Huxley destroyed, not my essay, but even this its short last sentence ?

His answer to my proposition that assumes him to hold " that all organisms consist alike of the same life-matter," is only that it turns on the ambiguity of the word " same." Will it be possible to make this good, however? Does Mr Huxley try it? Or is the reference to Whately enough for that? As for the word " same," I do not believe it to occur more than twice or thrice throughout the whole essay: identity is the term I use for the most part. I have no objection to the word, however, and think it perfectly justifiable: identity itself is certainly sameness. But more—I shall accept Mr Huxley's reference to the authority of Archbishop Whately in regard to it, and the ambiguity of its *two* senses. Of these, the primary one is that of numerical sameness, " applicable," says Whately, " to a single object;" as, I wore to-day the same boots I wore yesterday, meaning, of course, the same individual boots. In reference to the secondary one, again, the Archbishop's words are these:— " When several objects are undistinguishably alike, *one single description* will apply equally to any of them; and thence they are said to be all of *one and the same* nature, appearance, etc.: as *e.g.* when we say, this house is built of the *same* stone with such another, we only mean that the stones are undistinguishable in their qualities; not that the one building was pulled down, and the other constructed with the materials." Now, this latter sense is the sense in which Mr Huxley, I, and everybody else, for the most part, use the word; but whether Mr Huxley, I, or anybody else use the word, the context will always show if it be the rarer, primary, numerical sense that is intended or not. Does Mr Huxley insinuate that I represent him as arguing that the protoplasm of this monkey is *numerically* the same as the protoplasm of that man? I feel sure that it is impossible for either of us to be so absurd. But if he does not mean that, what *can* he mean by the ambiguity he flourishes, and his reference to Archbishop Whately? Whatever he means, I take him at his word; I tell him that, when he holds all living things to consist of the " same " protoplasm, " same " is not to him the term as used in Whately's primary, but as used in Whately's secondary sense; I tell him also that as it is to him, so it is to me. According to Whately, when we say, " this house is built of the same *stone* with such another, we merely mean that the *stones* are undistinguishable in their qualities:" similarly Mr Huxley, when he said that all life was built of the same *protoplasm*, meant it to be understood that the *protoplasms* were "undistinguishable in their qualities;" and—using words quite in his own sense—it was *that* I denied. Ambiguity there was none, and Archbishop Whately, Mr Huxley's own reference, but proves my case. Consider one or two of Mr Huxley's own phrases! " There is such *a* thing as *a* physical basis or matter of life;" . . . . or " *the* physical basis or matter of life." There is " a single physical basis of life," and through its unity " the whole living world " is pervaded by " a three-fold unity " —" namely, a unity of power or faculty, a unity of form, and a unity of substantial composition." With such expressions ringing in our ears—and they occur on every page—which of us, Mr Huxley or I, shall be said to be the one who rather *pushes* identity?

Omitting the deep logical question that lies at the bottom of all, may I not say, then, that my whole argument is a completely valid and scientific one, founded on scientific difference as opposed to Mr Huxley's argument from scientific identity? And, in short, in attempting to stamp out all essential differences in the one *non-existent* identity of a vital *matter*, has not Mr Huxley simply deluded himself? If I only hold up, then, the *difference* he *ignores* to the *identity* he *proclaims*, that is much more than the " ambiguity " of the word " same."

In answer to my proposition which speaks of " life-matter " as, in Mr Huxley's belief, "due only to chemistry," Mr Huxley affirms " statement number (2) is, in my judgment, absurd; and certainly I have never said anything resembling it." One is pleased to think that Mr Huxley has now come to consider such an opinion " absurd," but—" *certainly I have never said anything resembling it!*" Mr Huxley, for aught I know, may have some quibble in his mind about the phrase " due to chemistry;" but he has always, and everywhere, for all that, described his " life-matter as due to chemistry," and here are a few examples :—

" If the properties of water may be properly said to result from the nature and disposition of its component molecules, I can find no intelligible ground for refusing to say that the properties of protoplasm result from the nature and disposition of its molecules."

Is it possible for words more definitely to convey the statement that the properties of water and protoplasm are precisely on the same level, and that as the former are of molecular (physical, chemical) origin, so are the latter? Again, after having told us that protoplasm is carbonic acid, water, and ammonia, " which certainly possess no properties but those of ordinary matter," he proceeds to speak as follows : —

" Carbon, hydrogen, oxygen, and nitrogen are all lifeless bodies. Of these carbon and oxygen unite in certain proportions and under certain conditions, to give rise to carbonic acid ; hydrogen and oxygen produce water ; nitrogen and hydrogen give rise to ammonia. These new compounds, like the elementary bodies of which they are composed, are lifeless."

So far then, surely, I am allowed to say that these new compounds are *due* to chemistry. Observe now what follows :—

" But when they " (the compounds) " are brought together, under certain conditions, they give rise to the still more complex body, protoplasm, and this protoplasm exhibits the phenomena of life. I see no break in this series of steps in molecular complication, and I am unable to understand why the language which is applicable to any one term of the series, may not be used to any of the others."

Here, evidently, I am *ordered* by Mr Huxley himself, not to change my language, but to characterise these latter results as I characterised those former ones. If I spoke then of ammonia, etc., as due to chemistry, so must I now speak of protoplasm, life-matter, as due to chemistry—a statement which Mr Huxley not only orders *me* to make, but makes *himself*. Very curious all this, then. When I do what he bids me do, when I say what he says—that if ammonia, etc., are due to chemistry, protoplasm is also due to chemistry—Mr Huxley turns round and calls out that I am saying an "absurdity," which he, for his part, "certainly never said!" But let me make just one other quotation :—

"When hydrogen and oxygen are mixed in a certain proportion, and an electric spark is passed through them, they disappear, and a quantity of water equal in weight to the sum of their weights appears in their place."

Now, no one in his senses will dispute that this is a question of chemistry, and of nothing but chemistry; but it is Mr Huxley himself who asks in immediate and direct reference here :—

"Is the case in any way changed when carbonic acid, water, and ammonia disappear, and in their place, under the influence of pre-existing living protoplasm, an equivalent weight of the matter of life makes its appearance ?"

Surely Mr Huxley has no object whatever here but to place before us the genesis of protoplasm, and surely also this genesis is a purely chemical one! The very "influence of pre-existing living protoplasm,"—which *pre-existence* could not itself exist for the benefit of the *first* protoplasm that came into existence,—is asserted to be in precisely the same case with reference to the one process as that of the electric spark with reference to the other. And yet, in the teeth of such passages, Mr Huxley feels himself at liberty to say now, "statement number (2) is, in my judgment, absurd, and *certainly I have never said anything resembling it.*" It is a pity to see a man in the position of Mr Huxley so strangely *forget* himself!

Mr Huxley's next charge of "utter misrepresentation" on my part is, that I have talked of him as *founding* materialism, while it was "one great object" with him to *resist* it! I have been quite explicit everywhere as to Mr Huxley's *double* issue; but in the passage he refers to, I have only his first issue in consideration, as is the pitch of my essay in its first form generally indeed, and as—is perfectly well known to Mr Huxley. To attempt to hide his *first* issue from himself, then,—he can hide it from nobody else—by thrusting his head into the second, is but the sagacity of the ostrich. Seeing, however, that he resents my want of complete and formal analysis of the second or philosophical part of his essay, I have, in this edition, added it.

It is not every gentleman who allows himself so lightly such heavy weapons as " utter misrepresentations ; " and I can only say, as regards them all, that I am really sorry Mr Huxley should have so indulged himself.

Let it be borne in mind, too, that Mr Huxley's critique, as above resisted, applies not to my essay, but to its short last sentence ; which sentence, by the bye, happens (though I by no means disown, but completely homologate it) to have been a mere *addition* to the *proof* of my manuscript. Even so, he who reads again said last sentence, will find Mr Huxley's objections not only to be but word-deep—mere catch-words, then,—but to glance from the surface, without a scratch.

Passing now, then, from these three main and summarising objections of Mr Huxley's, I shall consider the others, taking them as they come in the extract, but, as said, in a course upwards.

The first that so comes concerns the nettle hair. I shall have contented myself, it seems, with taking my facts " at second hand." " A most amusing example," etc. . . . . " but why in the world did not this distinguished Hegelian look at a nettle hair for himself ? " Now, my single action being only to oppose difference to identity, I contend that, if, of the nettle hair, Stricker said A while Huxley said B, I had a perfect warrant to point out as much—let my own results of examination of the nettle hair have been what they might, and for the obvious reason that the known Stricker was an *authority*, whereas I, unknown, was none. But all that is beside the point, and I seize Mr Huxley here in the act, as is usual with him in my case, of mere word-catching. I do *not* meet Mr Huxley's description of the protoplasm of the nettle hair by Stricker's description in the same reference. My action, on the contrary, is this : To Mr Huxley's description of protoplasm *in general*, I oppose Stricker's description of protoplasm equally *in general*, and I point to the difference between them. Mr Huxley will probably exclaim, But it was the protoplasm of the nettle hair *I* described ! To this my answer is, Yes ; but you immediately proceeded, and at great length, to identify all protoplasm with that of the nettle hair ; and, therefore, I was perfectly warranted in assuming your description of the protoplasm of the nettle hair in the first instance, to be your description also of protoplasm in general and in all instances.   Reference to a sentence or two will prove this :—" Not the sting only," Mr Huxley tells us, " but the whole substance of the nettle is made up of a *repetition* of *such* masses of nucleated protoplasm."   Further, possession is expressly inferred " by many other organic forms" of such protoplasm as is possessed by the nettle ; and when he talks of " the comparison of such a protoplasm to a body with an internal circulation," " put forward by an eminent physiologist," he has no idea whatever, he says, of *confining* this comparison to the protoplasm of the nettle sting.   He says also: "Currents similar to those of the hairs of the nettle have been observed in a great multitude of very different plants, and weighty authorities have suggested that they probably occur in more or less perfection in all young vegetable cells."   And, immediately thereafter, in a burst of poetry as exuberant as the very vegetation he describes, he proceeds as follows :—"If such be the case, the *wonderful noonday silence* of a *tropical forest* is, after all, due only to *the dulness of our hearing* ; and could our ears catch the *murmurs* of these *tiny Maelstroms*, as they whirl in the *innumerable myriads* of living cells which constitute each tree, we should be *stunned* as with the *roar* of a *great city.*"   Surely there is here an extension ample enough to warrant me in assuming Mr Huxley to believe the same description to apply to protoplasm in general, which applied to the nettle hair in particular. But the main interest turned on *circulation :* that Stricker denied to exist in protoplasm in general.   Was I wrong, then, in an argument that sought only an accumulation of differences, to quote, as opposing Mr Huxley's so unexceptive authority *for* circulation, Stricker's equally decided authority *against* it ? Why, too, should Mr Huxley cry shame on me for adducing the evidence of *authorities*, and not of my *own eyes ?*   Had he himself not already set me the example ?   What are these " weighty authorities" he alludes to, and what is the effect of them ?   Is not that effect to " commend the poisoned chalice to his own lips ? "   " Why in the world did not this distinguished " Biologist " look for himself" at all these " young vegetable cells" and " tropical forests," " before venturing to speak a word about the matter at all ? "

But I have not yet given Mr Huxley's description of protoplasm one half the extension he himself gives it.   " The protoplasm of Algæ and Fungi," he tells us, "exhibits movements of its whole mass." Further still, he asserts of these phenomena that, "so far as they have been studied," "they are the same for the animal as for the plant." He says also of the white corpuscles of the blood, "The substance which is thus active is a mass of protoplasm, and its activity differs in detail, rather than in principle, from that of the protoplasm of the nettle." Then, "beast and fowl, reptile and fish, mollusc, worm, and polype, are all composed of structural units of the same character, namely, masses of protoplasm with a nucleus." Lastly, read this :—"The *nettle* arises, as the *man* does, in a mass of nucleated protoplasm!" After such enormous extension of the analogy of the nettle hair on the part of Mr Huxley, I really do not think I have any reason to apologise to him for regarding his description of nettle protoplasm as applicable to protoplasm in general, and for opposing to his expressions in that reference, Stricker's in the same. Mr Huxley, then, must consent to be self-convicted, not only of incautious word-catching here, but of being his own "most amusing example," for, as we have already seen, he appeals to *authorities*, when he might have used *his own eyes*.

Mr Huxley's next stroke of the knife, so far as attempt goes, is :—

"Dr Stirling has not taken the trouble to refer to the original authorities for his history, which is consequently a travesty."

One sees how much the "history" sticks in Mr Huxley's gorge! The authorities I specially name, however, are Rindfleisch, Kühne, and Stricker ; these, surely, are original authorities (though necessarily not all the original authorities in existence), for they have all contributed something (Kühne is about the greatest living name) to the actual march of the science in question ; and, surely also, they are, historically, the very strongest authorities that it is possible to mention. These three names I have used as vouchers for the correctness of my narrative ; are we to understand that Mr Huxley impugns *them*? Stricker's "Handbuch," to which I "*especially*" refer, is now in English ; and all, or all but all, the testimony I can possibly need will be found there. There indeed, *substantially*, is the same history that I have given ; shall we understand Mr Huxley to call this "history" a "travesty,"—on the part of "his valued friend, Professor Stricker?" "*Substantially*" I say, and reference to *sources* on my part has been frank from the first. Nevertheless, this "*substantially*" does not wholly deny to me all grounds for complacency in my own *work*, and in regard to facts that were then for the first time communicated to Englishmen. But more, though I referred to these three names only as my supporting authorities for the history in question, that "history" itself, beginning with Hunter, passes through the names of Schleiden, Müller, Brown, Valentin, Schwann, Virchow, Leydig, Bergmann, Haeckel, Dujardin, Remak, and, alluding to Meyen, Siebold, Reichert, Ecker, Henle, Kölliker, Beale, Huxley, and John Goodsir, ends with—to my mind, the three greatest and latest names in this connection—Brücke, Kühne, and Max Schultze. Now, though—and like Mr Huxley, I am *professionally* educated —I cannot profess to have read *all* the works this list indicates (who can ?), yet surely, if in view of nothing but said education, I must have read *some* of them,* and surely these are *the* "original authorities !" On that head I appeal to my own referees, and as to the meagre half-dozen names mentioned by Mr Huxley in his *rival* history, I would not think it desirable to admit into my own history a single one of them, unless, perhaps, that of Cohn. Mr Huxley opines that "Dr Stirling's method of dealing with the subject is peculiar." I rather think, however, that my reader will now *transfer* the stricture, and wonder at the power of countenance that could lead any man to say "travesty" in such a case.

I have now to thank Mr Huxley for having read my essay "with much interest." Interest on his part in any writing of mine I must hold to be a distinguished compliment. All the more, then, is my regret that "much of it" should remain as "dark" to him as "does the 'Secret of Hegel.'" Perhaps it may be natural in me, with my own progeny before me, to wonder how this should be in either case, but I cannot omit acknowledging the singular *good nature and loyalty* of the reference in the latter of them. Still, somehow, I have that confidence in the excellent faculty of Mr Huxley, that I must think he does himself injustice here. I cannot believe my essay not to have proved sun-clear to him everywhere, unless in the *wee,*

* Surely I *may* have consulted all of them—I ought to add, perhaps. At least it is not usual for one medical brother to deny another the freedom of the guild. Elsewhere, of course, Mr Huxley has so good a right to be proud of his own possession of "a nettle and a microscope," that I cannot resent his denial of "those not rare articles" to me.

wee bit into which the word *idea* entered, for a moment, with a somewhat Hegelian shade. Might I venture to hint, too, that Mr Huxley, if he still honours me with his interest, may find every difficulty in all these references dispelled in the popular statement (only fifteen pages long) of my first lecture on the Philosophy of Law?

I have given my reader the opportunity of seeing for himself every direct word that concerns me in Mr Huxley's essay, and I know but a single indirect one. That, too, I shall not withhold; it is this. The words immediately preceding the direct ones I have extracted, refer to " quite superfluous explosions on the part of some who should have been better informed" (then follow, as already quoted, "Dr Stirling, *for example*," etc.); and perhaps I shall not be wrong in taking this as an intimation on Mr Huxley's part, that *I* (the " for example") should have been " better informed." Well, it is a consummation always devoutly to be wished; but where, may I be allowed to ask, ought I, in *this* matter, to be " better informed?" That protoplasm, for example, was no longer an infinite variety of different cells, but an indifferent one material, as it were, in web? Well—perhaps so—but how then about the Germans? Really, *where* ought I in *this* matter to be better informed?—but no! I will not press farther this rhetorical hack! I will not as much as speak of Mr Huxley's poetry—of giant Californian pines and Indian figs—no! not even of the "great Finner whale, hugest of beasts that live, or have lived, disporting his eighty or ninety feet of bone, muscle, and blubber, *with easy roll*, among waves in which the stoutest ship that ever left dockyard," etc. Did my reader ever hear of " the great ring-tailed bab-boon from "—— But no!—I will refrain. Mr Huxley writes always an excellent clear English, and he does not generally yield to the charlatanism of the platform.

It would probably be now in place for me, as against such serious charges as "travesty " and " utter misrepresentation," to bring forward the counter-testimony of other experts of equal, or perhaps higher, rank than even Mr Huxley. This, too, I will now forego. I will refer only to Beale, Bastian, Gamgee, to Dr John Brown, to Dr Hodge of Princeton; and I will quote, in allusion to my essay, this single sentence from Sir John Herschel :—

" *Anything more complete and final in the way of refutation than this Essay, I cannot well imagine.*"

On the whole, perhaps it would have been as well if Mr Huxley had not found it necessary to say anything more in this matter, whether for " his own," or for or against anybody else. At all events, " travesty " and " utter misrepresentation " return straight home to the nest that hatched them.

In a business reference, perhaps I may be allowed to add that I sincerely apologise to the public for the length of time this little essay (though republished in America) has been kept out of print in Great Britain. That I was not the blameable cause of this admits of an easy explanation. The public, too, will perhaps kindly excuse the augmented price of the present edition in consideration of the increase of matter it contains, as well as of the fact that, at the price put upon it, the first edition did not pay expenses. The very convincing proof of this is that my late very liberal publishers, though they sold an edition of 750 copies in a few months, found it necessary not only to divide nothing, but to apply to me for three-and-fi'pence, which had been expended in postage stamps.

J. HUTCHISON STIRLING.

MARCH, 1872.

AS REGARDS PROTOPLASM, Etc.

—o✷o—

PART I.

THE FIRST (PHYSIOLOGICAL) ISSUE; OR THE "PLUNGE" INTO THE "MATERIALISTIC SLOUGH."

IT is a pleasure to perceive Mr Huxley open his clear little essay with what we may hold, perhaps, to be the manly and orthodox view of the character and products of the French writer, Auguste Comte. "In applying the name of 'the new philosophy' to that estimate of the limits of philosophical inquiry which he" (Professor Huxley), "in common with many other men of science, holds to be just," the Archbishop of York confounds, it seems, this new philosophy with the Positive philosophy of M. Comte; and thereat Mr Huxley expresses himself as greatly astonished. Some of us, for our parts, may be inclined at first to feel astonished at Mr Huxley's astonishment; for the school to which, at least on the philosophical side, Mr Huxley seems to belong, is even notorious for its prostration before Auguste Comte, whom, especially so far as method and systematisation are concerned, it regards as the greatest intellect since Bacon. For such, as it was the opinion of Mr Buckle, is understood to be the opinion also of Messrs Grote, Bain, and Mill. In fact, we may say that such is commonly and currently considered the characteristic and distinctive opinion of that whole perverted or inverted reaction which has been called the *Revulsion*. That is to say, to give this word a moment's explanation, that the Voltaires and Humes and Gibbons having long enjoyed an immunity of sneer at man's blind pride and wretched superstition—at *his* silly non-natural honour and *her* silly non-natural virtue—a reaction had set in, exulting in poetry, in the splendour of nature, the nobleness of man, and the purity of woman, from which reaction again we have, almost within the last decennium, been revulsively, as it were, called back,—shall we say by some "bolder" spirits—the Buckles, the

Mills, etc.?—to the old illumination or enlightenment of a hundred years ago, in regard to the weakness and stupidity of man's pretensions over the animality and materiality that limit him. Of this revulsion, then, as said, a main feature, especially in England, has been prostration before the vast bulk of Comte; and so it was that Mr Huxley's protest in this reference, considering the philosophy he professed, had that in it to surprise at first. But if there was surprise, there was also pleasure; for Mr Huxley's estimate of Comte is undoubtedly the right one. "So far as I am concerned," he says, "the most reverend prelate" (the Archbishop of York) "might dialectically hew M. Comte in pieces as a modern Agag, and I should not attempt to stay his hand; for, so far as my study of what specially characterises the Positive philosophy has led me, I find therein little or nothing of any scientific value, and a great deal which is as thoroughly antagonistic to the very essence of science as anything in ultramontane Catholicism." "It was enough," he says again, "to make David Hume turn in his grave, that here, almost within earshot of his house, an instructed audience should have listened without a murmur while his most characteristic doctrines were attributed to a French writer of fifty years' later date, in whose dreary and verbose pages we miss alike the vigour of thought and the exquisite clearness of style of the man whom I make bold to term the most acute thinker of the eighteenth century—even though that century produced Kant."

Of the doctrines themselves which are alluded to here, I shall say nothing now; but of much else that is said, there is only to be expressed a hearty and even gratified approval. I demur, to be sure, to the exaltation of Hume over Kant—high as I place the former. Hume, with infinite fertility, surprised us, it may be said, perhaps, into attention on a great variety of points which had hitherto passed unquestioned; but, even on these points, his success was of an interrupted, scattered, and inconclusive nature. He set the world adrift, but he set man too, reeling and miserable, adrift with it. Kant, again, with gravity and reverence, desired to refix, but in purity and truth, all those relations and institutions which alone give value to existence—which alone *are* humanity, in fact—but which Hume, with levity and mockery, had approached to shake. Kant built up again an entire new world for us of knowledge and duty, and, in a certain way, even belief; whereas Hume had sought to dispossess us of every support that man as man could hope to cling to. In a word, with at *least* equal fertility, Kant was, as compared with Hume, a graver, deeper, and so to speak, a more consecutive, more comprehensive spirit. Graces there were indeed, or even, it may be, subtleties, in which Hume had the advantage perhaps.

He is still in England an unsurpassed master of expression—this, certainly, in his History, if in his Essays he somewhat baffles his own self by a certain laboured breadth of conscious fine writing, often singularly inexact and infelicitous. Still Kant, with reference to his products, must be allowed much the greater importance. In the history of philosophy he will probably always command as influential a place in the modern world as Socrates in the ancient; while, as probably, Hume will occupy at best some such position as that of Heraclitus or Protagoras. Hume, nevertheless, if unequal to Kant, must, in view at once of his own subjective ability and his enormous influence, be pronounced one of the most important of writers. It would be difficult to rate too high the value of his French predecessors and contemporaries as regards purification of their oppressed and corrupt country; and Hume must be allowed, though with less call, to have subserved some such function in the land we live in. In preferring Kant, indeed, I must be acquitted of any undue partiality; for all that appertains to personal bias was naturally, and by reason of early and numerous associations, on the side of my countryman.

Demurring, then, to Mr Huxley's opinion on this matter, and postponing remark on the doctrines to which he alludes, I must express a hearty concurrence with every word he utters on Comte. In him I too "find little or nothing of any scientific value." I too have been lost in the mere mirage and sands of "those dreary and verbose pages;" and I acknowledge in Mr Huxley's every word the ring of a genuine experience. M. Comte was certainly a man of some mathematical and scientific proficiency, as well as of quick but biassed intelligence. A member of the *Aufklärung*, he had seen the immense advance of physical science since Newton, under, as is usually said, the method of Bacon; and, like Hume, like Reid, like Kant, *who had all anticipated him in this*, he sought to transfer that method to the domain of mind. In this he failed; and though in a sociological aspect he is not without true glances into the present disintegration of society and the conditions of it, anything of importance cannot be claimed for him. There is not a sentence in his book that, in the hollow elaboration and windy pretentiousness of its build, is not an exact type of its own constructor. On the whole, indeed, when we consider the little to which he attained, the empty inflation of his claims, the monstrous and maniacal self-conceit into which he was *exalted*, it may appear, perhaps, that charity to M. Comte himself, to say nothing of the world, should induce us to wish that both his name and his works were buried in oblivion. Now, truly, that Mr Huxley (the "call" being for the moment his) has so pronounced himself, especially as the facts of the case are exactly and absolutely what he indicates, perhaps we may expect this consummation not to be so very long delayed. More than those members of the revulsion already mentioned, one is apt to suspect, will be anxious now to beat a retreat. Not that this, however, is so certain to be allowed them; for their estimate of M. Comte is a valuable element in our estimate of them.

Frankness on the part of Mr Huxley is not limited to his opinion of M. Comte; it accompanies us throughout his whole essay. He seems even to take pride, indeed, in naming always and everywhere his object at the plainest. That object, in a general point of view, relates, he tells us, solely to materialism, but with a double issue. While it is his declared purpose, in the first place, namely, to lead us into materialism, it is equally his declared purpose, in the second place, to lead us out of materialism. On the first issue, for example, he directly warns his audience that to accept the conclusions which he conceives himself to have established on protoplasm, is to accept these also: That "all vital action" is but "the result of the molecular forces" of the physical basis; and that, by consequence, to use his own words to his audience, "the thoughts to which I am now giving utterance, and your thoughts regarding them are but the expression of molecular changes in that matter of life which is the source of our other vital phenomena." And, so far, I think, we shall not disagree with Mr Huxley when he says that "most undoubtedly the terms of his propositions are distinctly materialistic." Still, on the second issue, Mr Huxley asserts that he is "individually no materialist." "On the contrary, he believes materialism to involve grave philosophical error;" and the "union of materialistic terminology with the repudiation of materialistic philosophy" he conceives himself to share "with some of the most thoughtful men with whom he is acquainted." In short, to unite both issues, we have it in Mr Huxley's own words, that it is the single object of his essay "to explain how such a union is not only consistent with, but necessitated by, sound logic;" and that, accordingly, he will, in the first place, "lead us through the territory of vital phenomena to the materialistic slough," while pointing out, in the second, "the sole path by which, in his judgment, extrication is possible." Mr Huxley's essay, then, falls evidently into two parts; and of these two parts we may say, further, that while the one—that in which he leads us into materialism—will be predominatingly physiological, the other— or that in which he leads us out of materialism—will be predominatingly philosophical. Two corresponding parts would thus seem to be prescribed to any full discussion of the essay; and of these, in the present needs of the world, it is evidently the latter that has the more promising theme. The truth is, however, that Mr Huxley, after having exerted all his strength in his first part to throw us into "the materialistic slough," by *clear necessity of knowledge*, only calls to us, in his second part, cheerily, as it were, to come out of this slough again, on the somewhat *obscure necessity of ignorance*. This, then, is but a lop-sided balance, where a scale in the air only seems to struggle vainly to raise its well-weighted fellow on the ground. Mr Huxley, in fact, possesses no remedy for materialism but what lies in the expression that, while he knows not what matter is in itself, he certainly knows that causality is but contingent succession; and thus, like the so-called "philosophy" of the Revulsion, Mr Huxley would only mock us into the intensest dogmatism on the one side by a fallacious reference to the intensest scepticism on the other.

The present paper, then, will regard mainly Mr Huxley's argument *for* materialism, but say what is required, at the same time, on his alleged argument—which is merely the imaginary, or imaginative, impregnation of ignorance—*against it.**

Following Mr Huxley's own steps in his essay, the course of his positions will be found to run, in summary, thus :—

What is meant by the physical basis of life is, that there is one kind of matter common to all living beings, and it is named protoplasm. No doubt it may appear at first sight that, in the various kinds of living beings, we have only *difference* before us, as in the lichen on the rock and the painter that paints it,—the microscopic animalcule or fungus and the Finner whale or Indian fig—the flower in the hair of a girl and the blood in her veins, etc. Nevertheless, throughout these and all other diversities, there really exists a threefold *unity*: a unity of faculty, a unity of form, and a unity of substance.

On the first head, for example, or as regards faculty, power, the action exhibited, there are but three categories of *human* activity—contractility, alimentation, and reproduction; and there are no fewer for the *lower* forms of life, whether animal or vegetable. In the nettle, for instance, we find the woody case of its sting lined by a granulated, semi-fluid layer, that is possessed of contractility. But in this respect—that is, in the possession of contractile substance—other plants are as the nettle, and all animals are as plants. Protoplasm—for the nettle-layer alluded to is protoplasm—is common to the whole of them. The difference, in short, between the powers of the

* Mr Huxley's own extraordinary charge of "utter misrepresentation" in the above reference, has necessitated (in this edition) the present Part II., in express consideration of what Mr Huxley says "*against*" materialism. This essay is thus now quite too large, as compared with the one that gave rise to it—if quite too small on the other hand, for the matter (especially philosophical), it attempts in the end to discuss—a matter which has interest, perhaps, beyond Mr Huxley's reference.

lowest plant or animal and those of the highest is one only of degree and not of kind.

But, on the second head, it is not otherwise in form, or external appearance and manifested structure. Not the sting only, but the whole nettle, is made up of protoplasm; and of all the other vegetables the nettle is but a type. Nor are animals different. The colourless blood-corpuscles in man and the rest are identical with the protoplasm of the nettle; and both he and they consisted at first only of an aggregation of such. Protoplasm is the common constituent—the common origin. At last, as at first, all that lives, and every part of all that lives, are but nucleated or unnucleated, modified or unmodified, protoplasm.

But, on the third head, or with reference to unity of substance, to internal composition, chemistry establishes this also. All forms of protoplasm, that is, consist alike of carbon, hydrogen, oxygen, and nitrogen, and behave similarly under similar reagents.

So, now, a uniform character having in this threefold manner been proved for protoplasm, what is its origin, and what is its fate? Of these the latter is not far to seek. The fate of protoplasm is death—death into its chemical constituents; and this determines its origin also. Protoplasm can originate only in that into which it dies,—the elements—the carbon, hydrogen, oxygen, and nitrogen — of which it was found to consist. Hydrogen, with oxygen, forms water; carbon, with oxygen, carbonic acid; and hydrogen, with nitrogen, ammonia. Similarly, water, carbonic acid, and ammonia form, in union, protoplasm. The influence of pre-existing protoplasm only determines combination in *its* case, as that of the electric spark determines combination in the case of water. Protoplasm, then, is but an aggregate of physical materials, exhibiting in combination— only as was to be expected—new properties. The properties of water are not more different from those of hydrogen and oxygen than the properties of protoplasm are different from those of water, carbonic acid, and ammonia. We have the same warrant to attribute the consequences to the premises in the one case as in the other. If, on the first stage of combination, represented by that of water, *simples* could unite into something so different from themselves, why, on the second stage of combination, represented by that of protoplasm, should not *compounds* similarly unite into something equally different from themselves? If the constituents are credited with the properties *there*, why refuse to credit the constituents with the properties *here*? To the constituents of protoplasm, in truth, any new element, named vitality, has no more been added, than to the constituents of water any new element, named aquosity. Nor is there any logical halting-place between this conclusion and the further and final one: That all vital action whatever, intellectual included, is but the result of the molecular forces of the protoplasm which displays it.

These sentences will be acknowledged, I think, *at least* fairly to represent Mr Huxley's relative deliverances, and, consequently, as I may be allowed to explain again, the only important—while much the larger—part of the whole essay. Mr Huxley, that is, while devoting fifty paragraphs to our physiological immersion in the "materialistic slough," grants but one-and-twenty towards our philosophical escape from it; the fifty besides being, so to speak, in reality the wind, and the one-and-twenty only the whistle for it. What these latter say, in effect, is no more than this, that—matter being known not in itself but only in its qualities, and cause and effect not in their nexus, but only in their sequence,—matter may be spirit or spirit matter, cause effect or effect cause—in short, for aught that Mr Huxley more than phenomenally knows, this may be that or that this, first second, or second first, but the conclusion shall be this, that he will lay out all our *knowledge* materially, and we may lay out all our *ignorance* immaterially—if we will. Which reasoning and conclusion, I may merely remark, come precisely to this: That Mr Huxley—who, hoping yet to see each object (a pin, say) not in its qualities but in *itself*, still, consistently antithetic, cannot believe in the extinction of fire by water or of life by the rope, for any *reason* or for any *necessity* that lies in the nature of the case, but simply for the habit of the thing—has not yet put himself at home with the metaphysical categories of *substance* and *causality;* thanks, perhaps, to those guides of his whom we, the amusing Britons that we are, bravely proclaim "the foremost thinkers of the day !"*

The matter and manner of the whole essay are now fairly before us, and I think that, with the approbation of the reader, its procedure, generally, may be described as an attempt to establish, not by any complete and systematic induction, but by a variety of partial and illustrative assertions, two propositions. Of these propositions the first is, That all animal and vegetable organisms are essentially alike in power, in form, and in substance; and the second, That all vital and intellectual functions are the properties of the molecular disposition and changes of the material basis (protoplasm) of which the various animals and vegetables consist. In both propositions, the agent of proof is this same alleged material basis of life, or protoplasm. For the first proposition, all animal and vegetable organisms shall be identified in protoplasm; and for the second, a simple

* See note page 21.

chemical analogy shall assign intellect and vitality to the molecular constituents of the protoplasm, in connection with which they are at least exhibited.

In order, then, to obtain a footing on the ground offered us, the first question we naturally put is, What is Protoplasm? And an answer to this question can be obtained only by a reference to the historical progress of the physiological cell theory.

That theory may be said to have wholly grown up since John Hunter wrote his celebrated work *On the Nature of the Blood*, etc. New growths to Hunter depended on an exudation of the plasma of the blood, in which, by virtue of its own *plasticity*, vessels formed, and conditioned the further progress. The influence of these ideas seems to have still acted, even after a conception of the cell was arrived at. For starting element, Schleiden required an intracellular plasma, and Schwann a structureless exudation, in which minute granules, if not indeed already pre-existent, formed, and by aggregation grew into nuclei, round which singly the production of a membrane at length enclosed a cell. It was then that, in this connection, we heard of the terms blastema and cyto-blastema. The theory of the vegetable cell was completed earlier than that of the animal one. Completion of this latter, again, seems to have been first effected by Schwann, after Müller had insisted on the analogy between animal and vegetable tissue, and Valentin had demonstrated a nucleus in the animal cell, as previously Brown in the vegetable one. But assuming Schwann's labour, and what surrounded it, to have been a first stage, the wonderful ability of Virchow may be said to have raised the theory of the cell fully to a second stage. Now, of this second stage, it is the dissolution or resolution that has led to the emergence of the word Protoplasm.

The body, to Virchow, constituted a free state of individual subjects, with equal rights but unequal capacities. These were the cells, which consisted each of an enclosing membrane, and an enclosed nucleus with surrounding intracellular matrix or matter. These cells, further, propagated themselves, chiefly by partition or division; and the fundamental principle of the whole theory was expressed in the dictum, " *Omnis cellula e cellula.*" That is, the nucleus, becoming gradually elongated, at last parted in the midst ; and each half, acting as centre of attraction to the surrounding intracellular matrix or contained matter, stood forth as a new nucleus to a new cell, formed by division at length of the original cell.

The first step taken in resolution of this theory was completed by Max Schultze, preceded by Leydig. This was the elimination, on the whole, of an investing membrane. Such membrane may, and does, ultimately form; but in the first instance, for the most part, it appears, the cell is naked. The second step in the resolution belongs perhaps to Brücke, though preceded by Bergmann, and though Max Schultze, Kühne, Haeckel, and others ought to be mentioned in the same connection. This step was the elimination, or at least subordination, of the nucleus. The nucleus, we are to understand now, is necessary, it may be, neither to the division nor to the existence of the cell.

Thus, then, stripped of its membrane, relieved of its nucleus, what now remains for the cell? Why, nothing but what *was* the contained matter, the intracellular matrix, and *is*—Protoplasm.

In the application of this word itself, however, to the element in question, there are also a step or two to be noticed. The first step was Dujardin's discovery of sarcode; and the second the introduction (by Mohl) of the term protoplasm as the name for the layer of the *vegetable* cell that lined the cellulose, and enclosed the nucleus. Sarcode, found in certain of the lower forms of life, was a simple substance that exhibited powers of spontaneous contraction and movement. Thus, processes of such simple, soft, contractile matter are protuded by the rhizopods, and locomotion by their means effected. Remak first extended the use of the term protoplasm from the layer which bore that name in the vegetable cell to the analogous element in the animal cell; but it was Max Schultze, in particular, who, by applying the name to the intracellular matrix, or contained matter, when divested of membrane, and by identifying this substance itself with sarcode, first fairly established protoplasm, name and thing, in its present prominence.

In this account I have necessarily omitted many subordinate and intervening steps in the successive establishment, apparently, of the *contractility*, superior *importance*, and complete *isolation* of this thing to which, under the name of protoplasm, Mr Huxley of late has called such vast attention. Besides the names mentioned, there are others of great eminence in this connection, such as Meyen, Siebold, Reichert, Ecker, Henle, and Kölliker among the Germans; and among ourselves, Beale and Huxley himself. John Goodsir will be mentioned again.

We have now, perhaps, obtained a general idea of protoplasm. Brücke, when he talks of it as "living cell-body or elementary organism," comes very near the leading idea of Mr Huxley as expressed in his phrase, "the physiological basis, or matter, of life." Living cell-body, elementary organism, primitive living matter—that, evidently, is the quest of Mr Huxley. There is aqueous matter, he would say, perhaps, composed of hydrogen and oxygen, and it is the same thing whether in the rain-drop

or the ocean ; so, similarly, there is vital matter, which, composed of carbon, hydrogen, oxygen, and nitrogen, is the same
thing whether in cryptogams or in elephants, in animalcules or
in men.   What, in fact, Mr Huxley seeks, probably, is living
protein—protein, so to speak, struck into life. Just such appears
to him to be the nature of protoplasm, and in it he believes
himself to possess at last *a living clay* wherewith to build the
whole organic world.

The question, What is Protoplasm ? is answered, then ; but,
for the understanding of what is to follow, there is still one
general consideration to be premised.

Mr Huxley's conception of protoplasm, as we have seen, is
that of living matter, living protein ; what we may call, perhaps, elementary life-stuff.   Now, is it quite certain that Mr
Huxley is correct in this conception ?   Are we to understand,
for example, that cells have now definitively vanished, and left
in their place only a uniform and universal *matter* of quite in-
definite proportions?   No ; such an understanding would be
quite wrong.   Whatever may be the opinion of the adherents
of the molecular theory of generation (namely, that physical
molecules combine of themselves into living organisms), it is
certain that all the great German histologists still hold by the
cell, and can hardly open their mouths without mention of it.
I do not allude here to any special adherents of either nucleus
or membrane, but to the most advanced innovators in both
respects ; to such men as Schultze and Brücke and Kühne.
These, as we have seen, pretty well confine their attention, like
Mr Huxley, to the protoplasm.   But they do not the less on that
account talk of the cell.   For them, it is only in cells that protoplasm exists.   To their view, we cannot fancy protoplasm as
so much matter in a pot, in an ointment-box, any portion of
which scooped out in an ear-picker would be so much life-stuff,
and, though a part, quite as good as the whole.   This seems to
be Mr Huxley's conception, but it is not theirs.   A certain
measure goes with protoplasm to constitute it an organism to
them, and worthy of their attention.   They refuse to give consideration to any mere protoplasm-*shred* that may not have yet
ceased, perhaps, to exhibit all sign of contractility under the
microscope, and demand a protoplasm-*cell*.   In short, protoplasm is to them still distributed in cells, and only that measure
of protoplasm is cell that is adequate to the whole group of
vital manifestations.   Brücke, for example, of all innovators
probably the most innovating, and denying, or inclined to deny,
both nucleus and membrane, does not hesitate, according to
Stricker, to speak still of cells as self-complete organisms, that
move and grow, that nourish and reproduce themselves, and
that perform specific function.   " Omnis cellula e cellula," is the

rubric they work under as much now as ever. The heart of a turtle, they say, is not a turtle; so neither is a protoplasm-shred a protoplasm-cell.

This, then, is the general consideration which I think it necessary to premise; and it seems, almost of itself, to negate Mr Huxley's reasonings in advance, for it warrants us in denying that physiological clay of which all living things are but bricks baked, Mr Huxley intimates, and in establishing in its place cells as before—living cells that differ infinitely the one from the other, and so differ from the very first moment of their existence. This consideration shall not be allowed to pretermit, however, an examination of Mr Huxley's own proofs, which will only the more and more avail to indicate the difference suggested.

These proofs, as has been said, would, by means of the single fulcrum of protoplasm, establish first, the identity, and second, the materiality of all life, whether vegetable or animal. These are, shortly, the two propositions which we have already seen, and to which, in their order, we now pass.

All organisms then, whether animal or vegetable, have been understood for some time back to originate in and consist of cells; but the progress of physiology has *seemed* now to substitute for cells a single matter of life, protoplasm; and it is here that Mr Huxley, rather too precipitately, perhaps, sees his cue. Mr Huxley's very first word is the "physical basis or matter of life;" and he supposes (in his advanced knowledge), " that to many the idea that there is such a thing may be novel." This then, so far, is, though a misunderstanding, what is *new* in Mr Huxley's contribution. He seems to have said to himself, if formerly the whole world was thought kin in an "ideal" or formal element, organisation, I shall now, by (supposed) aid of the Germans, finally complete this identification in a "physical" or material element, protoplasm. In short, what at this stage we are asked to witness in the essay is, the identification of all living beings whatever in the identity of protoplasm. As there is a single matter, clay, which is the matter of all bricks, so there is a single matter, protoplasm, which is the matter of all organisms. "Protoplasm is the clay of the potter, which, bake it and paint it as he will, remains clay, separated by artifice, and not by nature, from the commonest brick or sun-dried clod." Now here I cannot help stopping a moment to remark that Mr Huxley puts emphatically his whole soul into this sentence, and evidently believes it to be, if we may use the word, a *clincher*. But, after all, does it say much? or rather, does it say anything? To the question, "Of what are you made?" the answer, for a long time now, and by the great mass of human beings who are supposed civilised, has been "Dust." Dust, and the same dust, has been allowed to constitute us all. But materialism has not on that account been the irresistible result. Attention hitherto —and surely excusably, or even laudably in such a case—has been given not so much to the dust as to the " potter," and the " artifice" by which he could so transform, or, as Mr Huxley will have it, *modify* it. To ask us to say clay, or even proto-plasm, instead of dust, is not to ask us for much, then, seeing that even to Mr Huxley there still remain both the " potter" and his " artifice."

But to return: To Mr Huxley, when he says all bricks, being made of clay, are the same thing, we answer, Yes, undoubtedly, if they are made of the same clay. That is, the bricks are identical if the clay is identical; but, on the other hand, by as much as the clay differs will the bricks differ. And, similarly, all organisms can be identified only if their composing proto-plasm can be identified. To this stake is the argument of Mr Huxley tied.

This argument itself takes, as we have seen, a threefold course: Mr Huxley will prove his position in this place by reference, firstly, to unity of faculty; secondly, to unity of form; and thirdly, to unity of substance. It is this course of proof, then, which we have now to follow, but taking the question of substance, as simplest, first, and the others later.

By substance, Mr Huxley understands the internal or chemi-cal composition; and, with a mere reference to the action of reagents, he asserts the protoplasm of all living beings to be an identical combination of carbon, hydrogen, oxygen, and nitro-gen. It is for us to ask, then, Are all samples of protoplasm identical first, in their chemical composition, and, second, under the action of the various reagents?

On the first clause, we may say, in the first place, towards a proof of difference which will only cumulate, I hope, that, even should we grant in all protoplasm an identity of chemical in-gredients, what is called *Allotropy* may still have introduced no inconsiderable variety. Ozone is not antozone, nor is oxy-gen either, though in chemical constitution all are alike. In the second place, again, we may say that, with *varying pro-portions*, the same component parts produce very various results. By way of illustration, it will suffice to refer to such different things as the proteids, gluten, albumen, fibrin, gelatine, &c., compared with the urinary products, urea and uric acid; or with the biliary products, glycocol, glycocholic acid, bili-rubin, bili-verdin, &c.; and yet all these substances, varying so much the one from the other, are, as protoplasm is, compounds of carbon, hydrogen, oxygen, and nitrogen. But, in the third place, we are not limited to a *may say*; we can assert the fact that all protoplasm is not chemically identical. All the tissues of the

organism are called protoplasm by Mr Huxley; but can we predicate chemical identity of muscle and bone, for example? In
such cases Mr Huxley, it is true, may bring the word "modified"
into use; but the objection of modification we shall examine
later. In the meantime, we are justified, by Mr Huxley's very
argument, in regarding all organised tissues whatever as protoplasm; for if these tissues are not to be identified in protoplasm,
we must suppose denied what it was his one business to affirm.
And it is against that affirmation that we point to the fact of
much chemical difference obtaining among the tissues, not only
in the *proportions* of their fundamental elements, but also in the
addition (and proportions as well) of such others as chlorine,
sulphur, phosphorus, potass, soda, lime, magnesia, iron, etc.
Vast differences vitally must be legitimately assumed for tissues
that are so different chemically. But, in the fourth place, we
have the authority of the Germans for asserting that the cells
themselves—and they now, to the most advanced, are only
protoplasm—do differ chemically, some being found to contain
glycogen, some cholesterine, some protagon, and some myosin.
Now such substances, let the chemical analogy be what it may,
must still be allowed to introduce chemical difference. In the
last place, Mr Huxley's analysis is an analysis of *dead* protoplasm, and indecisive, consequently, for that which lives. Mr
Huxley betrays sensitiveness in advance to this objection; for
he seeks to rise above both sensitiveness and objection at once
by styling the latter "frivolous." Nevertheless the Germans
say pointedly that it is unknown whether the same elements
are to be referred to the cells after as before death. Kühne
does not consider it proved that living muscle contains syntonin;
yet Mr Huxley tells us, in his Physiology, that "syntonin is the
chief constituent of muscle and flesh." In general, we may say,
according to Stricker, that all weight is put now on the examination of living tissue, and that the difference is fully allowed
between that and dead tissue.

On the second clause now, or with regard to the action of
reagents, these must be denied to produce the like result on the
various forms of protoplasm. With reference to temperature,
for example, Kühne reports the movements of the amoeba to be
arrested in iced water; while, in the same medium, the ova of
the trout furrow famously, but perish even in a warmed room.
Others, again, we are told, may be actually dried, and yet live.
Of ova in general, in this connection, it is said that they live or
die according as the temperature to which they are exposed
differs little or much from that which is natural to the organisms producing them. In some, according to Max Schultze,
even distilled water is enough to arrest movement. Now, not
to dwell longer here, both amoeba and ova are to Mr Huxley

pure protoplasm; and such difference of result, according to
difference of temperature, etc., must assuredly be allowed to
point to a difference of original nature. Any conclusion so far,
then, in regard to unity of substance, whether the chemical
composition or the action of reagents be considered, cannot be
said to bear out the views of Mr Huxley.

What now of the unities of form and power in protoplasm?
By form, Mr Huxley will be found to mean the general appearance and structure; and by faculty or power, the action
exhibited. Now it will be very easy to prove that, in neither
respect, do all specimens of protoplasm agree. Mr Huxley's
representative protoplasm, it appears, is that of the nettle-sting;
and he describes it as a granulated, semi-fluid body, contractile
in mass, and contractile also in detail to the development of a
species of circulation. Stricker, again, speaks of it as a homogeneous substance, in which any granules that may appear
must be considered of foreign importation, and in which there
are no evidences of circulation. In this last respect, then, that
Mr Huxley should talk of "tiny Maelstroms," such as even in
the silence of a tropical noon might stun us, if heard, as "with
the roar of a great city," may be viewed, perhaps, as a rise into
poetry—beyond the occasion.

Further, according to Stricker, protoplasm varies almost infinitely in consistence, in shape, in structure, and in function.
In consistence, it is sometimes so fluid as to be capable of form-
ing in drops; sometimes semi-fluid and gelatinous; sometimes
of considerable resistance. In shape—for to Stricker the cells
are now protoplasm—we have club-shaped protoplasm, globe-
shaped protoplasm, cup-shaped protoplasm, bottle-shaped protoplasm — spindle-shaped protoplasm — branched, threaded,
ciliated protoplasm — circle-headed protoplasm — flat, conical,
cylindrical, longitudinal, prismatic, polyhedral, and palisade-like
protoplasm. In structure, again, it is sometimes uniform and
sometimes reticulated into interspaces that contain fluid. In
function, lastly—and here we have entered on the consideration
of faculty or power—some protoplasm is vagrant (so to translate *wandernd*), and of unknown use, like the colourless blood-
corpuscles.—

(In reference to these, as strengthening the argument, and
throwing much light generally, I break off a moment to say that,
very interesting as they are in themselves, and as Recklinghausen,
in especial, has made them, Mr Huxley's theory of them dis-
agrees considerably with the prevalent German one. He speaks
of them as the source of the body in general, yet, in his Physiology, he talks of the spleen, the lymphatics, and even the liver
—*parts* of the body—as *their* source. They are so few in
number that, while Mr Huxley is thankful to be able to point

to the inside of the lips as a seat for them, they bear to the red corpuscles only the proportion of 1 to 450. This disproportion, however, is no bar to Mr Huxley's derivation of the latter from the former. But the fact is questioned. The Germans, generally, for their part, describe the colourless, or vagrant, blood-corpuscles as probably media of conjugation or reparation, but acknowledge their function to be as yet quite unknown; while Rindfleisch, characterising the spleen as the grave of the red, and the womb of the white, corpuscles, evidently refers the latter to the former. This, indeed, is a matter of direct assertion with Preyer, who has "shown that pieces of red blood-corpuscles may be eaten by the amoeboid cells of the frog," and holds that the latter (the white corpuscles) proceed directly from the former (the red corpuscles); so that it seems to be determined in the meantime that there is no proof of the reverse being the fact).

—In function, then, to resume, some protoplasm is vagrant, and of unknown use. Some again produces pepsine, and some fat. Some at least contains pigment. Then there is nerve-protoplasm, brain-protoplasm, bone-protoplasm, muscle-protoplasm, and protoplasm of all the other tissues, no one of which but produces only its own kind, and is uninterchangeable with the rest. Lastly, on this head, we have to point to the overwhelming fact that there is the infinitely different protoplasm of the various infinitely different plants and animals, in each of which its own protoplasm, as in the case of that of the various tissues, but produces its own kind, and is uninterchangeable with that of the rest.

It may be objected, indeed, that these latter are examples of modified protoplasm. The objection of modification, as said, we have to see by itself later; but, in the meantime, it may be asked, Where are we to begin, *not* to have modified protoplasm? We have the example of Mr Huxley himself, who, in the nettle-sting, begins already with modified protoplasm; and we have the authority of Rindfleisch for asserting that "in every different tissue we must look for a different initial term of the productive series." This, evidently, is a very strong light on the original multiplicity of protoplasm, which the consideration, as we have seen, of the various plants and animals, has made, further, infinite. This is enough; but there is no wish to evade beginning with the very beginning — with absolutely pure initial protoplasm, if it can but be given us in any reference. The simple egg—that, probably, is the beginning—that, probably, is the original identity; yet even there we find already distribution of the identity into infinite difference. This, certainly, with reference to the various organisms, but with reference also to the various tissues. That we regard the egg as the beginning, and that we do not start, like the smaller exceptional physiological school, with molecules themselves, and the assumption of their spontaneous combination into organised life, depends on this, that the great Germans so often alluded to, Kühne among them, still trust in the experiments of Pasteur; and while they do not deny the possibility, or even the fact, of molecular generation, still feel justified in denying the existence of any observation that yet unassailably attests a *generatio æquivoca* (the production of life without preceding life). By such authority as this the simple philosophical spectator has no choice but to take his stand; and therefore it is that I assume the egg as the established beginning, so far, of all vegetable and animal organisms. To the egg, too, as the beginning, Mr Huxley, though the lining of the nettle-sting is his representative protoplasm, at least refers. "In the earliest condition of the human organism," he says, in allusion to the white (vagrant) corpuscles of the blood, "in that state in which it has but just become distinguished from the egg in which it arises, it is nothing but an aggregation of such corpuscles, and every organ of the body was once no more than such an aggregation." Now, in beginning with the egg—an absolute beginning being denied us in consequence of the pre-existent infinite difference of the egg or eggs themselves—we may gather from the German physiologists some such account of the actual facts as this.

The first change signalised in the impregnated egg seems that of *Furchung*, or furrowing—what the Germans call the *Furchungskugeln*, the *Dotterkugeln*, form. Then these *Kugeln*—clumps, eminences, monticles, we may translate the word—break into cells; and these are the cells of the embryo. Mr Huxley, as quoted, refers to the whole body, and every organ of the body, as at first but an aggregation of colourless blood-corpuscles; but in the very statement which would render the identity alone explicit, the difference is quite as plainly implicit. As much as this lies in the word "organs," to say nothing of "human." The cells of the "organs," to which he refers, are even then uninterchangeable, and produce but themselves. The Germans tell us of the *Keimblatt*, the germ-leaf, in which all these organs originate. This *Blatt*, or leaf, is threefold, it seems; but even these folds are not indifferent. The various cells have their distinct places in them from the first. While what in this connection are called the epithelial and endothelial tissues spring respectively from the *upper* and *under* leaf, connective tissues, with muscle and blood, spring from the *middle* one. Surely in such facts we have a perfect warrant to assert the initial non-identity of protoplasm, and to insist on this, that, from the very earliest moment—even literally *ab ovo*—brain-cells only generate brain-cells, bone-cells, bone-cells, and so on.

These considerations on function all concern faculty or power; but we have to notice now that the characteristic and fundamental form of power is to Mr Huxley *contractility*. He even quotes Goethe in proof of contractility being the main power or faculty of *Man!* Nevertheless it is to be said at once that, while there are differences in what protoplasm *is* contractile, all protoplasm is not contractile, nor dependent on contractility for its functions. In the former respect, for example, muscle, while it is the contractile tissue special, is also to Mr Huxley protoplasm; yet Stricker asserts the inner construction of the contractile substance, of which muscle-fibre virtually consists, to be essentially different from contractile protoplasm. Here, then, we have the contractile *substance* proper "essentially different" from the contractile *source* proper. In the latter respect, again, we shall not call in the *un*contractile substances which Mr Huxley himself denominates protoplasm—bread, namely, roast mutton, and boiled lobster; but we may ask where—even in the case of a living body—is the contractility of white of egg? In this reference, too, we may remark that Kühne, who divides the protoplasm of the epidermis into three classes, has been unable to distinguish contractility in his own third class. Lastly, where, in relation to the protoplasm of the nervous system, is there evidence of its contractility? Has any one pretended that thought is but the contraction of the brain; or is it by contraction that the very nerves operate contraction—the nerves that supply muscles, namely? Mr Huxley himself, in his Physiology, describes nervous action very differently. There *conduction* is spoken of without a hint of contraction. Of the higher faculties of man I have to speak again; but let us just ask where, in the case of any pure sensation—smell, taste, touch, sound, colour—is there proof of any contraction? Are we to suppose that between the physical cause of heat without and the mental sensation of heat within, contraction is anywhere interpolated? Generally, in conclusion here, while reminding of Virchow's testimony to the inherent inequalities of cell-capacity, let us but, on the question of faculty, contrast the kidney and the brain, even as these organs are viewed by Mr Huxley. To him the one is but a sieve for the extrusion of refuse: the other thinks Newton's 'Principia' and Iliads of Homer.

Probably, then, in regard to any continuity in protoplasm of power, of form, or of substance, we have seen *lacunæ* enow. Nay, Mr Huxley himself can be adduced in evidence on the same side. Not rarely do we find in his essay admissions of *probability* where it is *certainty* that is alone in place. He says, for example, " It is more than probable that *when* the vegetable world *is* thoroughly explored we *shall* find all plants in possession of the same powers." When a conclusion is decidedly announced, it is rather disappointing to be told, as here, that the premises are still to collect. " *So far*," he says again, " as the conditions of the manifestations of the phenomena of contractility have *yet* been studied." Now, such a *so far* need not be *very far;* and we may confess in passing, that from Mr Huxley the phrase, " the conditions of the *manifestations* of the *phenomena*," grates. We hear again that it is " the rule *rather* than the exception," or that "weighty authorities have *suggested*" that such and such things " probably occur," or, while contemplating the nettle-sting, that such " *possible* complexity " in other cases "*dawns* upon one." On other occasions he expresses himself to the effect that " perhaps it would not yet be safe to say that *all* forms," etc. Nay, not only does he directly *say* that " it is by no means his intention to suggest that there is no difference between the lowest plant and the highest, or between plants and animals." but he directly proves what he says, for he demonstrates in plants and animals an *essential difference of power.* Plants *can* assimilate inorganic matters, animals can *not*, etc. Again, here is a passage in which he is seen to cut his own " *basis* " from beneath his own feet. After telling us that all forms of protoplasm consist of carbon, hydrogen, oxygen, and nitrogen " in very complex union," he continues, " To this complex combination, *the nature of which has never been determined with exactness*, the name of protein has been applied." This, plainly, is an identification, on Mr Huxley's own part, of protoplasm and protein; and what is said of the one being necessarily true of the other, it follows that Mr Huxley admits the nature of protoplasm never to have been determined with exactness, and that, even in his eyes, the *lis* is still *sub judice.* This admission is strengthened by the words, too, " If we use this term " (protein) " with such *caution* as may properly arise out of our *comparative ignorance* of the things for which it stands ; " which entitle us to demand, in consequence " of our comparative ignorance of the things for which it stands," " *caution* " in the use of the term protoplasm. In such a state of the case we cannot wonder that Mr Huxley's own conclusion here is: Therefore " all living matter is more or less albuminoid." All living matter is more or less albuminoid! That, indeed, is the single conclusion of Mr Huxley's whole industry; but it is a conclusion that, far from requiring the intervention of protoplasm, had been reached long before the word itself had been, in this connection, used.

It is in this way, then, that Mr Huxley can be adduced in refutation of himself; and I think his resort to an epigram of

Goethe's for reduction of the powers of man to those of contraction, digestion, and reproduction, can be regarded as an admission to the same effect. The epigram runs thus:—

> " Warum treibt sich das Volk so, und schreit ? Es will sich ernähren,
> Kinder zeugen, und die nähren so gut es vermag.
> Weiter bringt es kein Mensch, stell' er sich wie er auch will."

That means, quite literally translated, " Why do the folks make such a pother and stir ? They want to feed themselves, get children, and then feed them as best they can ; no man does more, let him do as he may." This, really, is Mr Huxley's sole proof for his classification of the powers of man. Is it sufficient? Does it not apply rather to the birds of the air, the fish of the sea, and the beasts of the field, than to man ? Did Newton only feed himself, beget children, and then feed them ? Was it impossible for him to do any more, let him do as he might? And what we ask of Newton we may ask of all the rest. To elevate, therefore, the passing whim of mere literary *Laune* into a cosmical axiom and a proof in place—this we cannot help adding to the other productions here in which Mr Huxley appears against himself.

But were it impossible either for him or us to point to these *lacunæ*, it would still be our right and our duty to refer to the present conditions of microscopic science in *general* as well as in *particular*, and to demur to the erection of its *dicta*, constituted as they yet are, into established columns and buttresses in support of any theory of life, material or other.

The most delicate and dubious of all the sciences, it is also the youngest. In its manipulations the slightest change may operate as a destructive drought, or an equally destructive deluge. Its very tools may positively create the structure it actually examines. The present state of the science, and what warrant it gives Mr Huxley to dogmatise on protoplasm, we may understand from this avowal of Kühne's : " To-day we believe that we see " such or such fact, " but know not that further improvements in the means of observation will not reveal what is assumed for certainty to be only illusion." With such authority to lean on—and it is the highest we can have—we may be allowed to entertain the conjecture, that it is just possible that some certainties, even of Mr Huxley, may yet reveal themselves as illusions.

But, in resistance to any sweeping conclusions built on it, we are not confined to a reference to the imperfections involved in the very nature and epoch of the science itself in *general*. With yet greater assurance of carrying conviction with us, we may point in *particular* to the actual opinions of its present professors. We have seen already, in the consideration premised, that Mr Huxley's hypothesis of a protoplasm *matter* is unsup-

ported, even by the most innovating Germans, who as yet will
not advance, the most advanced of them, beyond a protoplasm-
cell; and that his whole argument is thus sapped in advance.
But what threatens more absolute extinction of this argument
still, *all* the German physiologists do *not* accept even the *protoplasm*-cell. Rindfleisch, for example, in his recently published
" Lehrbuch der pathologischen Gewebelehre," speaks of the cell
very much as we understand Virchow to have spoken of it.
To him there is in the cell not only protoplasm but nucleus, and
perhaps membrane as well. To him, too, the cell propagates
itself quite as we have been hitherto fancying it to do, by
division of the nucleus, increase of the protoplasm, and ultimate
partition of the cell itself. Yet he knows withal of the opinions
of others, and accepts them in a manner. He mentions Kühne's
account of the membrane as at first but a mere physical limit
of two fluids—a mere peripheral film or curdling; still he
assumes a formal and decided membrane at last. Even Leydig
and Schultze, who shall be the express eliminators of the membrane—the one by initiation and the other by consummation—
confess that, as regards the cells of certain tissues, they have
never been able to detect in them the absence of a membrane.

As regards the nucleus again, the case is very much stronger.
When we have admitted with Brücke that certain cryptogam
cells, with Haeckel that certain protists, with Cienkowsky that
two monads, and with Schultze that one amoeba, are without
nucleus—when we have admitted that division of the cell *may*
take place without implicating that of the nucleus—that the
movements of the nucleus *may* be passive and due to those of
the protoplasm—that Baer and Stricker demonstrate the dis-
appearance of the original nucleus in the impregnated egg,—
when we have admitted this, we have admitted also all that can
be said in degradation of the nucleus. Even those who say all
this, still attribute to the nucleus an important and unknown *rôle*,
and describe the formation in the impregnated egg of a new
nucleus; while there are others again who resist every attempt
to degrade it. Böttcher asserts movement for the nucleus, even
when wholly removed from the cell; Neumann points to such
movement in dead or dying cells; and there is other testimony
to a like effect, as well as to peculiarities of the nucleus otherwise that indicate spontaneity. In this reference, we may allude
to the weighty opinion of the late Professor Goodsir, who anticipated in so remarkable a manner certain of the determinations
of Virchow. Goodsir, in that anticipation, wonderfully rich and
ingenious as he is everywhere, is perhaps nowhere more interesting and successful than in what concerns the nucleus. Of the
whole cell, the nucleus is to him, as it was to Schleiden, Schwann,
and others, the most important element. And this is the view to

which I, who have little business to speak, wish success. This universe is not an accidental cavity, in which an accidental dust has been accidentally swept into heaps for the accidental evolution of the majestic spectacle of organic and inorganic life. That majestic spectacle is a spectacle as plainly for the eye of reason as any diagram of mathematic. That majestic spectacle could have been constructed, *was* constructed, only in reason, for reason, and by reason. From beyond Orion and the Pleiades, across the green hem of earth, up to the imperial personality of man, all, the furthest, the deadest, the dustiest, is for fusion in the invisible point of the single Ego—*which alone glorifies it. For* the subject, and on the model of the subject, all is made. Therefore it is that—though precisely as there are acephalous monsters by way of exception and deformity, there may be also at the very extremity of animated existence cells without a nucleus—I cannot help believing that this nucleus itself, as analogue of the subject, will yet be proved the most important and indispensable of all the normal cell elements. Even the phenomena of the impregnated egg seem to me to support this view. In the egg, on impregnation, it seems to me natural (I say it with a smile) that the old sun that ruled it should go down, and that a new sun, stronger in the combination of the new and the old, should ascend into its place!

Be these things as they may, we have now overwhelming evidence before us for concluding, with reference to Mr Huxley's first proposition, that—in view of the nature of microscopic science—in view of the state of belief that obtains at present as regards nucleus, membrane, and entire cell—even in view of the supporters of protoplasm itself—Mr Huxley is not authorised to speak of a physical matter of life; which, for the rest, if granted, would, for innumerable and, as it appears to me, irrefragable reasons, be obliged to acknowledge for itself, not identity, but an infinite diversity in power, in form, and in substance.

So much for the first proposition in Mr Huxley's essay, or that which concerns protoplasm, as a supposed matter of life, identical itself, and involving the identity of all the various organs and organisms which it is assumed to compose. What now of the second proposition, or that which concerns the materiality at once of protoplasm, and of all that is conceived to derive from protoplasm? In other words, though, so to speak, for organic bricks anything like an organic clay still awaits the proof, I ask, if the bricks are not the same, because the clay is not the same, what if the materiality of the former is equally unsupported by the materiality of the latter? Or what if the functions of protoplasm are not the properties of its mere molecular constitution?

For this is Mr Huxley's second proposition, namely, That all
vital and intellectual functions are but the properties of the
molecular disposition and changes of the material basis (protoplasm) of which the various animals and vegetables consist.
With the conclusions now before us, it is evident that to enter
at all on this part of Mr Huxley's argumentation is, so far as we
are concerned, only a matter of grace. In order that it should
have any weight, we must grant the fact, at once of the existence of a matter of life, and of all organs and organisms being
but aggregates of it. This, obviously, we cannot now do. By
way of hypothesis, however, we may assume it. Let it be
granted, then, that *pro hac vice* there *is* a physical basis of life
with all the consequences named ; and now let us see how Mr
Huxley proceeds to establish its materiality.

The whole former part of Mr Huxley's essay consists (as said)
of fifty paragraphs, and the argument immediately concerned is
confined to the latter ten of them. This argument (see also
p. 22) is the simple chemical analogy that, under stimulus of an
electric spark, hydrogen and oxygen uniting into an equivalent
weight of water, and, under stimulus of pre-existing protoplasm,
carbon, hydrogen, oxygen, and nitrogen uniting into an equivalent weight of protoplasm, there is the same warrant for attributing the properties of the consequent to the properties of the
antecedents in the latter case as in the former. The properties
of protoplasm are, in origin and character, precisely on the same
level as the properties of water. The cases are perfectly parallel.
It is as absurd to attribute a new entity vitality to protoplasm,
as a new entity aquosity to water. Or, if it is by its mere
chemical and physical structure that water exhibits certain properties called aqueous, it is also by its mere chemical and
physical structure that protoplasm exhibits certain properties
called vital. All that is necessary in either case is, "under
certain conditions," to bring the chemical constituents together. If water is a molecular complication, protoplasm is
equally a molecular complication, and for the description of the
one or the other there is no change of language required. A
new substance with new qualities results in precisely the same
way here, as a new substance with new qualities there ; and the
derivative qualities are not more different from the primitive
qualities in the one instance, than the derivative qualities are
different from the primitive qualities in the other. Lastly, the
modus operandi of pre-existent protoplasm is not more unintelligible than that of the electric spark. The conclusion is irresistible, then, that all protoplasm being reciprocally convertible,
and consequently identical, the properties it displays, vitality
and intellect included, are as much the result of molecular constitution as those of water itself.

It is evident, then, that the fulcrum on which Mr Huxley's second proposition rests, is a single inference from a chemical analogy. Analogy, however, being never identity, is apt to betray. The difference it hides may be essential, that is, while the likeness it shows may be inessential—so far as the conclusion is concerned. That this mischance has overtaken Mr Huxley here, it will, I fancy, not be difficult to demonstrate.

The analogy to which Mr Huxley trusts has two references: one to chemical composition, and one to a certain stimulus that determines it. As regards chemical composition, we are asked, by virtue of the analogy obtaining, to identify, as equally simple instances of it, protoplasm here and water there; and, as regards the stimulus in question, we are asked to admit the action of the electric spark in the one case to be quite analogous to the action of pre-existing protoplasm in the other. In both references I shall endeavour to point out that the analogy fails; or, as we may say it also, that, even to Mr Huxley, it can only seem to succeed by discounting the elements of difference that still subsist.

To begin with chemical combination, it is not unjust to demand that the analogy which must be admitted to exist in that, and a general physical respect, should not be strained beyond its legitimate limits. Protoplasm cannot be denied to be a chemical substance; protoplasm cannot be denied to be a physical substance. As a compound of carbon, hydrogen, oxygen, and nitrogen, it comports itself chemically—at least in ultimate instance—in a manner not essentially different from that in which water, as a compound of hydrogen and oxygen, comports itself chemically. In mere physical aspect, again, it may count quality for quality with water in the same aspect. In short, so far as it is on chemical and physical structure that the possession of distinctive properties in any case depends, both bodies may be allowed to be pretty well on a par. The analogy must be allowed to hold so far; so far but no farther. One step farther and we see not only that protoplasm has, like water, a chemical and physical structure; but that, unlike water, it has also an organised or organic structure. Now this, on the part of protoplasm, is a possession in excess; and with relation to that excess there can be no grounds for analogy. This, perhaps, is what Mr Huxley has omitted to consider. When insisting on attributing to protoplasm the qualities it possessed, because of its chemical and physical structure, if it was for chemical and physical structure that we attributed to water *its* qualities, he has simply forgotten the addition to protoplasm of a third structure that can only be named organic. "If the phenomena exhibited by water are its properties, so are those presented by protoplasm, living or dead, its properties." When Mr Huxley speaks thus, Exactly so, we may answer: "living or dead"—

organic or inorganic! That alternative is simply slipped in and
passed; but it is in that alternative that the whole matter lies.
Chemically, dead protoplasm is to Mr Huxley quite as good as
living protoplasm. As a sample of the article, he is quite con-
tent with dead protoplasm, and even swallows it, he says, in
the shape of bread, lobster, mutton, etc., with all the satisfactory
results to be desired. We shall not grudge Mr Huxley his
bread, his lobster, or his mutton. Still, as concerns the argument, it must be pointed out that it is only these that (as inorganic) can be placed on the same level as water; and that living
protoplasm is not only unlike water, but it is unlike dead protoplasm. Living protoplasm, namely, is identical with dead
protoplasm only so far as its chemistry is concerned (if even so
far as that); and it is quite evident, consequently, that difference between the two cannot depend on that in which they are
identical—cannot depend on the chemistry. Life, then, is no
affair of chemical and physical structure, and must find its explanation in something else. It is thus that, lifted high enough,
the light of the analogy between water and protoplasm is seen
to go out. Water, in fact, when formed from hydrogen and
oxygen, is, in a certain way, and in relation to them, no new
product; it has still, like them, only chemical and physical
qualities; it is still, as they are, inorganic. So far as *kind* of
power is concerned, they are still on the same level. But not
so protoplasm, where, with preservation of the chemical and
physical likeness, there is the addition of the unlikeness of life,
of organisation, and of ideas. But the addition is a new world
—a new and higher world, the world of a self-realising thought,
the world of an *entelechy*. The change of language objected to by
Mr Huxley is thus a matter of necessity, for it is *not* mere molecular complication that we have any longer before us, and the
qualities of the derivative are essentially and absolutely different
from the qualities of the primitive. If we did invent the term
aquosity, then, as an abstract sign for all the qualities of water,
we should really do very little harm; but aquosity and vitality
would still remain essentially unlike. While for the invention
of aquosity there is little or no call, however, the fact in the
other case is that we are not only compelled to invent, but
to *perceive* vitality. We are quite willing to do as Mr Huxley
would have us to do: look on, watch the phenomena, and name
the results. But just in proportion to our faithfulness in these
respects is the necessity for the recognition of a new world and
a new nomenclature. It is possible, certainly, to object that
there are different *states* of water, as ice and steam. But the
relation of the solid to the liquid, or of either to the vapour,
surely offers no analogy to the relation of protoplasm dead to
protoplasm alive. That relation is not an analogy but an

antithesis. The antithesis of antitheses. In it, in fact, we are in presence of the one incommunicable gulf—the gulf of all gulfs—that gulf which Mr Huxley's protoplasm is as powerless to efface as any other material expedient that has ever been suggested since the eyes of men first looked into it—the mighty gulf between death and life.

The differences alluded to (they are, in order, 1, organisation and life, 2, the objective idea—design, and 3, the subjective idea—thought), it may be remarked, are admitted by those very Germans to whom protoplasm, name and thing, is due. They, the most advanced and innovating of them, directly avow that there is present in the cell " an architectonic principle that has not yet been detected." In pronouncing protoplasm capable of active or vital movements, they do by that refer, they admit also, to an immaterial force, and they ascribe the processes exhibited by protoplasm—in so many words—not to the molecules, but to organisation and life. It is pointed out by Kant generally, that the reason of the specific mode of existence of every part of a living body lies in the whole, whilst with dead masses each part bears this reason within itself; and this indeed is how the two worlds are differentiated. A drop of water, once formed, is there passive for ever, susceptible to influence, but indifferent to influence, and what influence reaches it is wholly from without. It may be added to, it may be substracted from; but infinitely apathetic quantitatively, it is qualitatively independent. It is indifferent to its own physical parts. It is without contractility, without alimentation, without reproduction, without specific function. Not so the cell, in which the parts are dependent on the whole, and the whole on the parts; which has its activity and *raison d'être* within; which manifests all the powers which we have described water to want; and which requires for its continuance conditions of which water is independent. It is only so far as organisation and life are concerned, however, that the cell is thus different from water. Chemically and physically, as said, it can show with it quality for quality. How strangely Mr Huxley's deliverances show beside these facts! He can "see no break in the series of steps in molecular complication;" but, glaringly obvious, there is a step added that is not molecular at all, and that has its supporting conditions completely elsewhere. The molecules are as fully accounted for in protoplasm as in water; but the sum of qualities, thus exhausted in the latter, is not so exhausted in the former, in which there are qualities due, plainly, not to the molecules as molecules, but to the form into which they are thrown, and the force that makes that form one. When the chemical elements are brought together, Mr Huxley says, protoplasm is formed, " and this protoplasm exhibits the phenomena of life;" but he ought to have added that these phenomena are themselves added to the phenomena for which all that relates to chemistry stands, and are there, consequently, only by reason of some other determinant. New consequents necessarily demand new antecedents. " We think fit to call different kinds of matter carbon, oxygen, hydrogen, and nitrogen, and to speak of the various powers and activities of these substances as the properties of the matter of which they are composed." That, doubtless, is true, we say; but such statements do not exhaust the facts. We call water hydrogen and oxygen, and attribute *its* properties to the properties of them. In a chemical point of view, we ought to do the same thing for ice and steam; yet, maugre the chemical identity of the three, water is not ice, nor is either steam. Do we, then, in these cases, make nothing of the *difference,* and in its despite enjoy the satisfaction of viewing the three as one? Not so; we ask a reason for the difference; we demand an antecedent that shall render the consequent intelligible. The chemistry of oxygen and hydrogen is not enough in explanation of the threefold form; and by the very necessity of the facts we are driven to the addition of heat. It is precisely so with protoplasm in its twofold form. The chemistry remaining the same in each (if it really does so), we are compelled to seek elsewhere a reason for the difference of living from dead protoplasm. As the differences of ice and steam from water lay not in the hydrogen and oxygen, but in the heat, so the difference of living from dead protoplasm lies not in the carbon, the hydrogen, the oxygen, and the nitrogen, but in the vital organisation. In all cases, for the new quality, plainly, we must have a new explanation. The qualities of a steam-engine are not the results of its simple chemistry. We do apply to protoplasm the same conceptions, then, that are legitimate elsewhere, and in allocating properties and explaining phenomena we simply insist on Mr Huxley's own distinction of "living or dead." That, in fact, is to us the distinction of distinctions, and we admit no vital action whatever, not even the dullest, to be the result of the *molecular* action of the protoplasm that displays it. The very protoplasm of the nettle-sting, with which Mr Huxley begins, is already vitally organised, and in that organisation as much superior to its own molecules as the steam-engine, in its mechanism, to its own wood and iron. It were indeed as rational to say that there is no principle concerned in a steam-engine or a watch but that of its molecular forces, as to make this assertion of organised matter. Still there are degrees in organisation, and the highest forms of life are widely different from the lowest. Degrees similar we see even in the inorganic world. The persistent flow of a river is, to the mighty reason of the solar system, in some such proportion, perhaps, as the rhizopod to man. In protoplasm, even the lowest, then, but much more conspicuously in the highest, there is, in addition to the molecular force, another force unsignalised by Mr Huxley—the force of vital organisation.

But this force is a rational unity, and that is an idea; and this I would point to as a *second* form of the addition to the chemistry and physics of protoplasm. We have just seen, it is true, that an idea may be found in inorganic matter, as in the solar and sidereal systems generally. But the idea in organised matter is not one operative, so to speak, from without; it is one operative from within, and in an infinitely more intimate and pervading manner. The units that form the complement of an inorganic system are but independently and externally in place, like units in a procession; but in what is organised there is no individual that is not sublated into the unity of the single life. This is so even in protoplasm. Mr Huxley, it is true, desiderates, as result of mere ordinary chemical process, a life-stuff in mass, as it were in the web, to which he has only to resort for cuttings and cuttings in order to produce, by aggregation, what organised individual he pleases. But the facts are not so: we cannot have protoplasm in the web, but the piece. There is as yet no *matter* of life; there are still *cells* of life. It is no shred of protoplasm—no spoonful or toothpickful—that can be recognised as adequate to the function and the name. Such shred may wriggle a moment, but it produces nought, and it dies. In the smallest, lowest protoplasm cell, then, we have this rational unity of a complement of individuals that only are for the whole and exist in the whole. This is an idea, therefore; this is design: the organised concert of many to a single common purpose. The rudest savage that should, as in Paley's illustration, find a watch, and should observe the various contrivances all controlled by the single end in view, would be obliged to acknowledge—though in his own way—that what he had before him was no mere physical, no mere molecular product. So in protoplasm: even from the first, but, quite undeniably, in the completed organisation at last, which alone it was there to produce; for a single idea has been its one manifestation throughout. And in what machinery does it not at length issue? Was it molecular powers that invented a respiration—that perforated the posterior ear to give a balance of air—that compensated the *fenestra ovalis* by a *fenestra rotunda* —that placed in the auricular sacs those *otolithes*, those express stones for hearing? Such machinery! The *chordæ tendineæ* are to the valves of the heart exactly adjusted check-strings; and the contractile *columnæ carneæ* are set in, under contraction and expansion, to equalise the length of these strings to their office. Membranes, rods, and liquids—it required the express experiment of man to make good the fact that the structure of the ear exhibited really the most perfect apparatus possible for the purpose. And are we to conceive such machinery, such apparatus, such contrivances merely molecular? Are molecules adequate to such things—molecules in their blind passivity, and dead, dull insensibility? Is it to molecular agency Mr Huxley himself owes that "singular inward laboratory" of which he speaks, and without which all the protoplasm in the world would be useless to him? Surely, in the presence of these manifest ideas, it is impossible to attribute the single peculiar feature of protoplasm—its vitality, namely—to mere molecular chemistry. Protoplasm, it is true, breaks up into carbon, hydrogen, oxygen, and nitrogen, as water does into hydrogen and oxygen; but the watch breaks similarly up into mere brass, and steel, and glass. The loose materials of the watch—even its chemical materials if you will—replace its weight, quite as accurately as the constituents, carbon, etc., replace the weight of the protoplasm. But neither these nor those replace the vanished idea, which was alone the important element. Mr Huxley saw no break in the series of steps in molecular complication; but, though not molecular, it is difficult to understand what more striking, what more absolute break could be desired than the break into an idea. It is of that break alone that we think in the watch; and it is of that break alone that we should think in the protoplasm which, far more cunningly, far more rationally, constructs a heart, an eye, or an ear. That is the break of breaks, and explain it as we may, we shall never explain it by molecules.

But, if inorganic elements as such are inadequate to account either for vital organisation or the objective idea of design, much more are they inadequate, in the *third* place, to account for the subjective idea, for the phenomena of thought as thought. Yet Mr Huxley tells us that thought is but the expression of the molecular changes of protoplasm. This he only tells us; this he does not prove. He merely says that, if we admit the functions of the lowest forms of life to be but "direct results of the nature of the matter of which they are composed," we must admit as much for the functions of the highest. We have not admitted Mr Huxley's presupposition; but, even with its admission, we should not feel bound to admit his conclusion. In such a mighty system of differences, there are ample room and verge enough for the introduction of new motives. We can say here at once, in fact, that as thought, let its connection be what it may with, has never been proved to result from, organisation, no improvement of the proof required will be found in protoplasm. No one power that Mr Huxley signalises in protoplasm can account for thought : not alimentation, and not reproduction, certainly ; but not even contractility. We have seen already that there is no proof of contraction being necessary even for the simplest sensation ; but much less is there any proof of a necessity of contraction for the inner and independent operations of the mind. Mr Huxley himself admits this. He says : "Speech, gesture, and every other form of human action are, in the long-run, resolvable into muscular contraction ;" and so, " even those manifestations of intellect, of feeling, and of will, which we rightly name the higher faculties, are not excluded from this classification, inasmuch as to every one *but the subject of them*, they are known only as transitory changes in the relative positions of parts of the body." The concession is made here, we see, that these manifestations are differently known to the subject of them. But we may first object that, if even that privileged " every one but the subject" were limited to a knowledge of contractions, he would not know much. It is only because he knows, first of all, a thinker and willer of contractions that these themselves cease to be but passing externalities, and transitory contingencies. Neither is it reasonable to assert an identity of nature for contractions, and for that which they only represent. It would hardly be fair to confound either the receiver or the sender of a telegraphic message, with the movements which alone bore it, and without which it would have been impossible. The sign is not the thing signified, it is but the servant of the signifier—his own arbitrary mark—and intelligible, in the first place, only to him. It is the meaning, in all cases, that is alone vital ; the sign is but an accident. To convert the internality into the arbitrary externality that simply expresses it, is for Mr Huxley only an oversight. Your ideas are made known to your neighbour by contractions, therefore your ideas are of the same nature as contractions ! Or, even to take it from the other side, your neighbour perceives in you contractions only, and therefore your ideas are contractions ! Are not the vital elements here present the two correspondent internalities, between which the contractions constitute but an arbitrary chain of external communication, that is so now, but may be otherwise again? The ringing of the bell at the window is not precisely the dwarf within. Nor are Engineer Chappe's " wooden arms and elbow-joints jerking and fugling in the air," to be identified with Engineer Chappe himself. For the higher faculties, even for speech, etc., assuredly Mr Huxley might have well spared himself this superfluous and inapplicable reference to contraction.

But, in the middle of it, as we have seen, Mr Huxley concedes that these manifestations are differently known to the subject of them. If so, what becomes of his assertion of but a certain number of powers for protoplasm? The manifestations of the higher faculties are not known to the subject of them by contraction, etc. By what, then, are they known? According to Mr Huxley, they can only be known by the powers of protoplasm; and therefore, by his own showing, protoplasm must possess powers other than those of his own assertion. Precisely, then, his one great power of contractility, Mr Huxley himself confesses to be inapplicable here. Indeed, in his Physiology (p. 193), he makes such an avowal as this:—" We class *sensations*, along with *emotions*, and *volitions*, and *thoughts* under the common head of states of *consciousness;* but what consciousness is we know not, and how it is that anything so remarkable as a state of consciousness comes about as the result of irritating nervous tissue, is just as unaccountable as the the appearance of the Djin when Alladin rubbed his lamp in the story." Consciousness plainly was not muscular contraction to Mr Huxley when he wrote his Physiology; it is only since then that he has gone over to the assertion of no power in protoplasm but the triple power, contractility, etc. But the truth is only as his Physiology has it—the cleft is simply, as Mr Huxley acknowledges it there, absolute. On one side there is the world of externality, where all is body by body, and away from one another—the boundless reciprocal exclusion of the infinite object. On the other side, there is the world of internality, where all is soul to soul, and away into one another—the boundless reciprocal inclusion of the infinite subject. This — even while it is true that, for subject to be subject, and object object, the boundless intussuscepted multiplicity of the single invisible point of the one, is but the dimensionless casket into which the illimitable Genius of the other must retract and withdraw itself—is the difference of differences; and certainly it is not internality that can be abolished before externality. The proof for the absoluteness of thought, the subject, the mind, is, on its side, pretty well perfect. It is not necessary here, however, to enter into that proof at length. Before passing on, I may simply point to the fact that, if thought is to be called a function of matter, it must be acknowledged to be a function wholly peculiar and unlike any other. In all other functions, we are present to processes which are in the same sense physical as the organs themselves. So it is with lung, stomach, liver, kidney, where every step can be followed, so to speak, with eye and hand; but all is changed when we have to do with mind as the function of brain. Then, indeed, as Mr Huxley thought in his Physiology, we are admitted, as if by touch of Aladdin's lamp, to a world absolutely different and essentially new—to a world, on its side of the incommunicable cleft, as complete, entire, independent, self-contained, and absolutely *sui generis*, as the world of matter on the other side. It will be sufficient here to allude to as much as this, with special reference to the fact that, so far as this argument is concerned, protoplasm has not introduced any the very slightest difference. All the ancient reasons for the independence of thought as against organisation, can be used with even more striking effect as against protoplasm; but it will be sufficient to indicate this, so much are the arguments in question a common property now. Thought, in fact, brings with it its own warrant; or it brings with it, to use the phrase of Burns, "its patent of nobility direct from Almighty God." And that is the strongest argument on this whole aspect. Throughout the entire universe, organic and inorganic, thought is the controlling sovereign; nor does matter anywhere refuse its allegiance. So it is in thought, too, that man has *his* patent of nobility, believes that he is created in the image of God, and knows himself a freeman of infinitude.

But the analogy, in the hands of Mr Huxley, has, we have seen, a second reference—that, namely, to the excitants, if we may call them so, which *determine* combination. The *modus operandi*, Mr Huxley tells us, of pre-existing protoplasm in determining the formation of new protoplasm, is not more unintelligible than the *modus operandi* of the electric spark in determining the formation of water; and so both, we are left to infer, are perfectly analogous. The inferential turn here is rather a favourite with Mr Huxley. "But objectors of this class," he says on an earlier occasion, in allusion to those who hesitate to conclude from dead to living matter, "do not seem to reflect that it is also, in strictness, true that we know nothing about the composition of any body whatever as it is." In the same neighbourhood, too, he argues that, though impotent to restore to decomposed calc-spar its original form, we do not hesitate to accept the chemical analysis assigned to it, and should not, consequently, any more hesitate because of any mere difference of form to accept the analysis of dead for that of living protoplasm. It is certainly fair to point out that, if we bear ignorance and impotence with equanimity in one case, we may equally so bear them in another; but it is not fair to convert ignorance into knowledge, nor impotence into power. Yet it is usual to take such statements loosely, and let them pass. It is not considered that, if we know nothing about the composition of any body whatever as it is, then we do know nothing, and that it is strangely idle to offer absolute ignorance as a support for the most dogmatic knowledge. If such statements are, as is really expected for them, to be accepted, yet not accepted, they are the stultification of all logic. Is the chemistry of living to be seen to be the same as the chemistry of dead protoplasm, because we know nothing about the composition of any body whatever as it is? We know perfectly well that black is white, for we are absolutely ignorant of either as it is! The *form* of the calc-spar, which we *can* analyse, we cannot restore; therefore the *form* of the protoplasm, which we *cannot* analyse, has nothing to do with the matter in hand; and the chemistry of what is dead may be accepted as the chemistry of what is living! In the case of reasoning so irrelevant it is hardly worth while referring to what concerns the forms themselves; that they are totally incommensurable, that in all forms of calc-spar there is no question but of what is physical, while in protoplasm the change of form is introduction into an entire new world. As in these illustrations, so in the case immediately before us. No appeal to ignorance in regard to something else, the electric spark, should be allowed to transform another ignorance, that of the action of pre-existing protoplasm, into knowledge, here into *the* knowledge that the two unknown things, because of non-knowledge, are—perfectly analogous! That this analogy does not exist—that the electric spark and pre-existing protoplasm are, in their relative places, *not* on the same chemical level—this is the main point for us to see; and Mr Huxley's allusion to our ignorance must not be allowed to blind us to it. Here we have in a glass vessel so much hydrogen and oxygen, into which we discharge an electric spark, and water is the result. Now what analogy is it possible to perceive between this production of water by external experiment and the production of protoplasm by protoplasm? The discrepancy is so palpable that it were impertinent to enlarge on it.* The truth is just this, that the measured and mixed gases, the vessel, and the spark, in the one case, are as unlike the fortuitous food, the living organs, and the long process of assimilation in the other case, as the product water is unlike the product protoplasm. No; that the action of the electric spark should be unknown, is no reason why we should not insist on protoplasm for protoplasm, on life for life. Protoplasm can only be produced by protoplasm, and each of all the innumerable varieties of protoplasm, only by its own kind. For the protoplasm of the worm we must go to the worm, and for that of the toad-stool to the toad-stool. In fact, if all living beings come from protoplasm, it is quite as certain that, but for living beings, protoplasm would disappear. Without an egg you cannot have a hen— that is true; but it is equally true that, without a hen, you cannot

---

* I point out below, however, as one instance of this discrepancy, that were the cases really analogous, the spark ought to produce not water, but itself. The Rev. Mr Martin, in an article in the "British and Foreign Evangelical Review" for Jan. 1870, adds (I do not quote his exact words)—"or the water ought to have been produced, not by a spark, but by water." I beg to thank Mr Martin for the suggestion, as well as for the great kindness that inspires his eloquent article.

have an egg. So in protoplasm; which consequently, in the production of itself, offers no analogy to the production, or precipitation by the electric spark, *not of itself*, but of water. Besides, if, for protoplasm, pre-existing protoplasm is always necessary, how was there ever a first protoplasm?

Generally, then, the analogy does not hold, whether in the one reference or the other, and Mr Huxley has no warrant for the reduction of protoplasm to the mere chemical level which he assigns it in either. That level is brought very prominently forward in such expressions as these: That it is only necessary to bring the chemical elements "together," "under certain conditions," to give rise to the more complex body, protoplasm, just as there is a similar expedient to give rise to water; and that, under the influence of pre-existing living protoplasm, carbonic acid, water, and ammonia disappear, and an equivalent weight of protoplasm makes its appearance, just as, under the influence of the electric spark, hydrogen and oxygen disappear, and an equivalent weight of water makes its appearance. All this, plainly, is to assume for protoplasm such mere chemical place and nature as consist not with the facts. The cases are, in truth, not parallel, and the "certain conditions" are wholly diverse. All that is said we can do at will for water, but nothing of what is said can we do at will for protoplasm. To say we can feed protoplasm, and so make protoplasm at will produce protoplasm, is very much, in the circumstances, only to say, and is not to say that, in this way, we make a chemical experiment. To insist on a chemical analogy, in fact, between water and protoplasm, is to omit the differences not covered by the analogy at all—thought, design, life, and all the processes of organisation; and it is but simple procedure to omit these differences only by an appeal to ignorance elsewhere.

It is hardly worth while, perhaps, to refer now again to the difference—here, however, once more incidentally suggested—between protoplasm and protoplasm. Mr Huxley, that is, almost in his very last word on this part of the argument (see page 38), seems to become aware of the bearing of this on what relates to materiality, and he would again stamp protoplasm (and with it life and intellect), into an indifferent identity. In order that there should be no break between the lowest functions and the highest (the functions of the fungus and the functions of man), he has "endeavoured to prove," he says, that the protoplasm of the lowest organisms is "essentially identical with, and most readily *converted* into that of any animal." On this alleged reciprocal *convertibility* of protoplasm, then, Mr Huxley would again found as well an inference of identity, as the further conclusion that the functions of the highest,

D

not less than those of the lowest animals, are but the molecular manifestations of their common protoplasm.

Is this alleged reciprocal *convertibility* true, then? Is it true that every organism can digest every other organism, and that thus a relation of identity is established between that which digests and whatever is digested? These questions place Mr Huxley's general enterprise, perhaps, in the most glaring light yet; for it is very evident that there is an end of the argument if all foods and all feeders are essentially identical both with themselves and with each other. The facts of the case, however, I believe to be too well known to require a single word here on my part. It is not long since Mr Huxley himself pointed out the great difference between the foods of plants and the foods of animals; and the reader may be safely left to think for himself of *ruminantia* and *carnivora*, of soft bills and hard bills, of molluscs and men. Mr Huxley talks feelingly of the possibility of himself feeding the lobster quite as much as of the lobster feeding him; but such pathos is not always applicable: it is not likely that a sponge would be to the stomach of Mr Huxley any more than Mr Huxley to the stomach of a sponge.

But a more important point is this, that the functions themselves remain quite apart from the alleged convertibility. We can neither acquire the functions of what we eat, nor impart our functions to what eats us. We shall not come to fly by feeding on vultures, nor they to speak by feeding on us. No possible manure of human brains will enable a corn-field to reason. But if functions are inconvertible, the convertibility of the protoplasm is idle. In this inconvertibility, indeed, functions will be seen to be independent of mere chemical composition. And that is the truth: for function there is more required than either chemistry or physics.

It is to be acknowledged—to notice a collateral but indispensable consideration, for the sake of completeness, and by way of transition to the final question of possible objections—that Mr Huxley would be very much assisted in his identification of differences, were but the theories of the molecularists, on the one hand, and of Mr Darwin, on the other, once for all established. The three modes of theorising indicated, indeed, are not without a tendency to approach one another; and it is precisely their union that would secure a definitive triumph for the doctrine of materialism. Mr Huxley, as we have seen—though what he desiderates is an autoplastic living *matter* that, produced by ordinary chemical processes, is yet capable of continuing and developing itself into new and higher forms—still begins with the egg. Now the theory of the molecularists would, for its part, remove all the difficulties that, for materialism, are involved in the necessity of an egg; it would place protoplasm, as formed from molecules, undeniably at length on a merely chemical level; and, his theory being sound, would fairly enable. Mr Darwin, supplemented by such a life-stuff, to account by natural means for everything like an idea or thought that appears in creation. The misfortune is, however, that we must believe the theory of the molecularists still to await the proof; while the theory of Mr Darwin has many difficulties peculiar to itself. This theory, philosophically, or in ultimate analysis, is an attempt to prove that design, or the objective idea, especially in the organic world, is developed *in time* by natural means. The time which Mr Darwin demands, it is true, is an infinite time; and he thus gains the advantage of his processes being allowed greater *clearness* for the understanding, in consequence of the *obscurity* of the infinite past in which they are placed, and of which it is difficult in the first instance to deny any possibility whatever. Still it remains to be asked, Are such processes credible in any time? What Mr Darwin has done in aid of his view is, first, to lay before us a knowledge of facts in natural history of surprising richness; and, second, to support this knowledge by an inexhaustible ingenuity of hypothesis in arrangement of appearances. Now, in both respects, whether for information or even interest, the value of Mr Darwin's contribution will probably always remain independent of the argument or arguments that might destroy his leading proposition; and it is with this proposition that we have here alone to do. As said, we ask only, Is it true that the objective idea, the design which we see in the organised world, is the result in infinite time of the necessary adaptation of living structures to the peculiarities of the conditions by which they are surrounded?

Against this theory, then, its own absolute generalisation may be viewed as our first objection. In ultimate abstraction, that is, the only agency postulated by Mr Darwin is time—infinite time; and as regards actually existent beings and actually existent conditions, it is hardly possible to deny any possibility whatever to infinitude. If told, for example, that the elephant, if only obliged *infinitely* to run, might be converted into the stag, how should we be able to deny? So also, if the lengthening of the giraffe's neck were hypothetically attributed to a succession of dearths in infinite time that only left the leaves of trees for long-necked animals to live on, we should be similarly situated as regards denial. Still it can be pointed out that ingenuity of natural conjecture has, in such cases, no less wide a field for the negation than for the affirmation; and that, on the question of fact, nothing is capable of being determined. But we can also say more than that—we can say that any fruitful application even of *infinite time* to the *general problem of difference* in the world is inconceivable. To explain all from an absolute beginning requires us to commence with nothing; but to this nothing time itself is an addition. Time is an entity, a something, a difference added to the original identity; whence or how came time? Time cannot account for its own self; how is it that there is such a thing as time? Then no conceivable brooding even of infinite time could hatch the infinitude of space. How is it there is such a thing as space? No possible clasps of time and space, further, could ever conceivably thicken into matter. How is it that there is such a thing as matter? Lastly, so far, no conceivable brooding, or even gyrating, of a single matter in time and space could account for the specification of matter—carbon, gold, iodine, etc.—as we see and know it. Time itself remaining unaccounted for, space, matter, and the whole inorganic world, thus appear impassive to the action even of infinite time; all *these* differences are incapable of being accounted for so.

But suppose no curiosity had ever been felt in this reference, which, though scientifically indefensible, is quite possible, how about the transition of the inorganic into the organic? Mr Huxley tells us that, for food, the plant needs nothing but its bath of smelling-salts. Suppose this bath now—a pool of a solution of carbonate of ammonia; can any action of sun, or air, or electricity, be conceived to develop a cell—or even so much lump-protoplasm—in this solution? The production of an initial organism in any such manner will not allow itself to be realised to thought. Then we have just to think for a moment of the vast differences into which, for the production of the present organised world, this organism must be distributed, to shake our heads and say we cannot well refuse anything to an infinite time, but still we must pronounce a problem of this reach hopeless.

It is precisely in conditions, however, that Mr Darwin claims a solution of this problem. Conditions concern all that relates to air, heat, light, land, water, and whatever they imply. Our second objection, consequently, is, that conditions are quite inadequate to account for present organised differences, from a single cell. Geological time, for example, falls short, after all, of infinite time; or, in known geological eras, let us calculate them as liberally as we may, there is not time enough to account for the presently-existing varieties, from one, or even several, primordial forms. So to speak, it is not *in* geological time to account for the transformation of the elephant into the stag from acceleration, or for that of the stag into the elephant from retardation, of movement. And we may speak similarly of the growth of the neck of the giraffe, or even of the elevation of the monkey into man. Moreover, time apart, conditions have no such power in themselves. It is impossible to conceive of animal or vegetable effluvia ever creating the nerve by which they are felt, and so gradually the Schneiderian membrane, nose, and whole olfactory apparatus. Yet these effluvia are the conditions of smell, and, *ex hypothesi*, ought to have created it. Did light, or did the pulsations of the air, ever by any length of time, indent into the sensitive cell, eyes, and a pair of eyes—ears, and a pair of ears? Light conceivably might shine for ever without such a wonderfully complicated result as an eye. Similarly, for delicacy and marvellous ingenuity of structure, the ear is scarcely inferior to the eye; and surely it is possible to think of a whole infinitude of those fitful and fortuitous air-tremblings, which we call sound, without indentation into anything whatever of such an organ.

A third objection to Mr Darwin's theory is, that the play of natural contingency in regard to the vicissitudes of conditions, has no title to be named *selection*. Naturalists have long known and spoken of the "influence of accidental causes;" but Mr Darwin was the first to apply the term *selection* to the action of these, and thus convert accident into design. The agency to which Mr Darwin attributes all the changes which he would signalise in animals is really the fortuitous contingency of brute nature; and it is altogether fallacious to call such process, or such non-process, by a term involving foresight and a purpose. We have here, indeed, only a metaphor wholly misapplied. The German writer who, many years ago, said "even the *genera* are wholly a prey to the changes of the external universal life," saw precisely what Mr Darwin sees, but it never struck him to style contingency selection. Yet, how dangerous, how infectious, has not this ungrounded metaphor proved! It has become a *principle*, a *law*, and been transferred by very genuine men into their own sciences of philology, physiology, and what not. People will wonder at all this by-and-by. But to point out the inapplicability of such a word to the processes of nature referred to by Mr Darwin, is to point out also the impossibility of any such contingencies proceeding, by graduated rise, from stage to stage, into the great symmetrical organic system—the vast plan—the grand harmonious whole—by which we are surrounded. This rise, this system, is really the objective idea; but it is utterly incapable of being accounted for by any such agency as natural contingency in geological, or infinite, or any time. And it is this which the word selection tends to conceal.

We may say, lastly, in objection, here, that, in the fact of "reversion" or "atavism," Mr Darwin acknowledges his own failure. We thus see that the species as species is something independent, and holds its own *insita vis naturæ* within itself.

Probably it is not his theory, then, that gives value to Mr Darwin's book; nor even his ready ingenuity, whatever interest it may lend: it is the material information it contains. The ingenuity, namely, verges somewhat on that Humian expedient of natural conjecture so copiously exemplified, on occasion of a few trite texts, in Mr Buckle. But that natural conjecture is always insecure, equivocal, and many-sided. It may be said that ancient warfare, for example, giving victory always to the personally ablest and bravest, must have resulted in the improvement of the race; or that, the weakest being always necessarily left at home, the improvement was balanced by deterioration; or that the ablest were necessarily the most exposed to danger, and so, etc., etc., according to ingenuity, *usque ad infinitum.* Trustworthy conclusion is not possible to this method, but only to the induction of facts, or to scientific demonstration.

Neither molecularists nor Darwinians, then, are able to level out the difference between organic and inorganic, or between genera and genera, or species and species. The differences persist despite of both; the distributed identity remains unaccounted for. Nor, consequently, is Mr Darwin's theory competent to explain the objective idea by any reference to time and conditions. Living beings do exist in a mighty chain from the moss to the man; but that chain, far from founding, is founded in the idea, and is not the result of any mere natural *growth* of this into that. That chain is itself the most brilliant stamp, the sign-manual, of design. On every ledge of nature, from the lowest to the highest, there is a life that is *its*,—a creature to represent it, reflect it—so to speak, pasture on it. The last, highest, brightest link of this chain is man; the incarnation of thought itself, which is the summation of this universe; man, that includes in himself all other links and their single secret—the personified universe, the subject of the world. Mr Huxley makes but small reference to thought; he only tucks it in, as it were, as a mere appendicle of course.

It may be objected, indeed—to reach the last stage in this discussion—that, if Mr Huxley has not disproved the conception of thought and life " as a something which works through matter, but is independent of it," neither have we proved it. But it is easy for us to reply that, if " *independent of*," means here " *unconnected with*," we have had no such object. We have had no object whatever, in fact, but to resist, now the extravagant assertion that all organised tissue, from the lichen to Leibnitz, is alike in faculty, and again the equally extravagant assertion that life and thought are but ordinary products of molecular chemistry. As regards the latter assertion, we have endeavoured to show that the processes of vital organisation (as self-production, etc.) belong to another sphere, higher than, and very different from, those of mechanical juxtaposition or chemical neutralisation; that life, then, is no mere product of matter as matter; that if no life can be pointed to independent of matter, neither is there any life-stuff independent of life; and that life, consequently, adds a new and higher force to chemistry, as chemistry a new and higher force to mechanics, etc. As for thought, the endeavour was to show that it was as independent on the one side as matter on the other, that it controlled, used, summed, and was the reason of matter. Thought, then, is not to be reached by any bridge from matter, that is a hybrid of both, and explains the connection. The relation of matter to mind is not to be explained as a transition, but as a *contrecoup*. In this relation, however, it is not the material, but the mental side, which the whole universe declares to be the dominant one.

As regards any objections to the arguments which we have brought against the identity of protoplasm, again, these will lie in the phrase, probably, " difference not of kind, but degree," or in the word " modification." The " phrase " may be now passed, for generic or specific difference must be allowed in protoplasm, if not for the overwhelming reason that an infinitude of various kinds exist in it, each of which is self-productive and uninterchangeable with the rest, then for Mr Huxley's own reason, that plants assimilate inorganic matter and animals only organic. As for the objection " modification," again, the same consideration of generic difference must prove fatal to it. This were otherwise, indeed, could but the molecularists and Mr Darwin succeed in destroying generic difference; but in this, as we have seen, they have failed. And this will be always so: who dogs identify, difference dogs him. It is quite a justifiable endeavour, for example, to point out the identity that obtains between veins and arteries on the one hand, as between these and capillaries on the other; but all the time the difference is behind us; and when we turn to look, we see, for circulation, the valves of the veins and the elastic coats of the arteries as opposed to one another, and, for irrigation, the permeable walls of the capillaries as opposed to both.

Generic differences exist then, and we cannot allow the word " modification " to efface them in the interest of the identity claimed for protoplasm. Brain-protoplasm is not bone-protoplasm, nor the protoplasm of the fungus the protoplasm of man. Similarly, it is very questionable how far the word " modification " will warrant us in regarding with Mr Huxley the " ducts, fibres, pollen, and ovules " of the nettle as identical with the protoplasm of its sting. Things that originate alike may surely eventuate in others which, chemically and vitally, far from being

mere modifications, must be pronounced totally different. Such
eventuation must be held competent to what can only be named
generic or specific difference.   The "child" is only "*father* of
the man*"—it is not the man; who, moreover, in the course of
an ordinary life, we are told, has totally changed himself, not
once, but many times, retaining at the last not one single
particle of matter with which he set out. Such eventuations,
whether called modifications or not, certainly involve essential
difference. And so situated are the "ducts, fibres, pollen, and
ovules" of the nettle, which, whether compared with the
protoplasm of the nettle-sting, or with that in which they
originated, must be held to have assumed, by their own actions,
indisputable differences, physical, chemical, and vital, or in form,
substance, and faculty.

Much, in fact, depends on definition here; and, in reference to
modification, it may be regarded as arbitrary when identity
shall be admitted to cease and difference to begin. There are
the old Greek puzzles of the Bald Head and the Heap, for
example. How many grains, or how many hairs, may we
remove before a heap of wheat is no heap, or a head of hair
bald? These concern quantity alone; but, in other cases,
bone, muscle, brain, fungus, tree, man, there is not only a
quantitative, but a qualitative difference; and in regard to
such differences, the word modification can be regarded as
but a cloak, under which identity is to be shuffled into difference, but remain identity all the same. The brick is but
modified clay, Mr Huxley intimates, bake it and paint it as
you may; but is the difference introduced by the baking and
painting to be ignored? Is what Mr Huxley calls the "artifice"
not to be taken into account, leave alone the "potter"? The
strong firm rope is about as exact an example of modification
proper—modification of the weak loose hemp—as can well be
found; but are we to exclude from our consideration the whole
element of difference due to the hand and brain of man? Not
far from Burns's Monument, on the Calton Hill of Edinburgh,
there lies a mass of stones which is potentially a church, the
former Trinity College Church. Were this church again realised,
would it be fair to call it a mere modification of the previous
stones? Look now to the egg and the full-feathered fowl.
Chaucer describes to us the cock, "hight chauntecleere," that
was to his "faire Pertelotte" so dear:—

> " His comb was redder than the fine corall,
> Embattled, as it were a castle-wall ;
> His bill was black, and as the jet it shone ;
> Like azure were his legges and his tone (toes) ;
> His nailes whiter than the lilie flour,
> And like the burned gold was his colour."

Would it be even as fair to call this fine fellow—comb,

wattles, spurs, and all—a modified yolk, as to call the church, but modified stones? If, in the latter case, an element of difference, altogether undeniable, seems to have intervened, is not such intervention at least quite as well marked in the former? It requires but a slight analysis to detect that all the stones in question are marked and numbered; but will any analysis point out within the shell the various parts that only need arrangement to become the fowl? Are the men that may take the stones, and, in a re-erected Trinity College Church, realise anew the idea of its architect, in any respect more wonderful than the unknown disposers of the materials of the fowl? That what realises the idea should, in the one case, be from without, and, in the other, from within, is no reason for seeing more modification and less wonder in the latter than the former. There is certainly no more reason for seeing the fowl in the egg, and as identical with the egg, than for seeing a re-built Trinity College Church as identical with its unarranged materials. A part cannot be taken for the whole, whether in space *or in time*. Mr Huxley misses this. He is so absorbed in the identity out of which, that he will not see the difference into which, progress is made. As the idea of the church has the stones, so the idea of the fowl has the egg, for its commencement. But to this idea, and in both cases, the terminal additions belong, quite as much as the initial materials. If the idea, then, add sulphur, phosphorus, iron, and what not, it must be credited with these not less than with the carbon, hydrogen, etc., with which it began. It is not fair to mutter modification, as if it were a charm to destroy all the industry of time. The protoplasm of the egg of the fowl is no more the fowl than the stones the church; and to identify, by juggle of a mere word, parts in time and wholes in time so different, is but self-deception. Nay, in protoplasm, as we have so often seen, difference is as much present at first as at last. Even in its germ, even in its initial identity, to call it so, protoplasm is already different, for it issues in differences infinite.

Omission of the consideration of difference, it is to be acknowledged, is not nowadays restricted to Mr Huxley. In the wonder that is usually expressed, for example, at Oken's *identification* of the skull with so many vertebræ, it is forgot that there is still implicated the wonder which we ought to feel at the unknown power that could, in the end, so *differentiate* them. If the cornea of the eye and the enamel of the teeth are alike but modified protoplasm, we must be pardoned for thinking more of the adjective than of the substantive. Our wonder is how, for one idea, protoplasm could become one thing here, and, for another idea, another so different thing there. We are more curious about the modification than the protoplasm. In the

difference, rather than in the identity, it is, indeed, that the
wonder lies. Here are several thousand pieces of protoplasm;
analysis can detect no difference in them. They are to us, let
us say, as they are to Mr Huxley, identical in power, in form,
and in substance; and yet on all these several thousand little
bits of apparently indistinguishable matter an element of difference so pervading and so persistent has been impressed, that,
of them all, not one is interchangeable with another! Each
seed feeds its own kind. The protoplasm of the gnat will no
more grow into the fly than it will grow into an elephant.
Protoplasm is protoplasm: yes, but man's protoplasm is man's
protoplasm, and the mushroom's the mushroom's. In short, it
is quite evident that the word modification, if it would conceal,
is powerless to withdraw, the difference; which difference,
moreover, is one of kind and not of degree.

This consideration of possible objections, then, is the last we
have to attend to; and it only remains to draw the general
conclusion. All animal and vegetable organisms are alike in
power, in form, and in substance, only if the protoplasm of
which they are composed is similarly alike; and the functions
of all animal and vegetable organisms are but properties of the
molecular affections of their chemical constituents, only if
the functions of the protoplasm, of which they are composed,
are but properties of the molecular affections of *its* chemical
constituents. In disproof of the affirmative in both clauses,
there has been no object but to demonstrate, on the one hand,
the infinite non-identity of protoplasm, and, on the other, the
dependence of its functions upon other factors than its molecular
constituents.

In short, the whole position of Mr Huxley, that all organisms
consist alike of the same life-matter, which life-matter is, for its
part, due only to chemistry, must be pronounced untenable—
nor less untenable the materialism he would found on it.

PART II.

The Second (Philosophical) Issue; or, The Escape from Materialism through the Modern Idealism of Ignorance.

IN his necessity to say something, if only for "his own," Mr Huxley, in reference to my phrase "the materialism he would found on it," remarks, "one great object of my Essay was to show that what is called 'materialism' has no sound philosophical basis!" The note of admiration I retain here is Mr Huxley's own, and I am humbly of opinion that it is more in place at the end of *my* sentence than at the end of *his*. At the end of his, namely, it intimates indignation that an express effort to resist, should be treated as an express effort to found, materialism. At the end of mine, again, it intimates surprise that Mr Huxley should seek to hide his alpha beneath his beta, and upbraid me for openly signalising alpha alone, whereas I equally openly signalised beta—though placing it on one side. If Mr Huxley does *two* things namely—attempts, first, to set up materialism,—attempts, second, to knock down materialism (see pages 20, 21, 23)—how can allusion to the materialism he sets up, guarded by an equal allusion to the materialism he knocks down, be an "utter misreprentation?" "One great object of my Essay," says Mr Huxley! Yes, truly; but what of the *other*—great, greater, and greatest—object? "Utter misrepresentation!" The only utter misrepresentation concerned here is—Pshaw! the whole thing is beneath speech.

Nevertheless, my previous, merely parenthetic, treatment of Mr Huxley's second issue shall now be completed by a consideration in detail. We are to understand, then, that what Mr Huxley claimed to have effected (physiologically) in fifty paragraphs—for materialism, he now claims equally to effect (philosophically) in one-and-twenty—against it; and the means to this are "the principles which the Archbishop of York holds up to reprobation." These, as it is easy to know, concern the so-called "limits of philosophical inquiry," and may be reduced to what Mr Huxley holds to be our *three ignorances:* our ignorance, namely, first, of *cause;* second, of *substance;* and, third, of *externality*, or an external world. The evangile, according to Mr Huxley, consequently, is that, lost by *knowledge*, we may be saved by *ignorance!* Indeed, it must be allowed that the whole matter stands there very clear, consistent, definite, irrefutable, satisfactory, before Mr Huxley's own consciousness. The progress of knowledge generally, he is sure, has been ever more and more towards the reduction of all phenomena into the series and successions of material antecedents and consequents; and there cannot be a doubt but that life, and will, and thought, must, in the end, be all similarly tucked in. *These*, too, *when* explained, will only be explained as "results of the disposition of material molecules." It does not follow, for all that, is Mr Huxley's further thought, that what is called materialism is true, or that "there is nothing in the world but matter, force, and necessity;" I indeed have reduced all, we may further figure him to say, into material terms, and connected all in material sequence; but this system of a world may conceivably lie all the same, so to speak, in the drop of water in the hollow of an Arab boy's hand. That is, firstly, I know not any necessity of connection in the phenomena of the world, though I know the fact of it; and so volition *may* be free. Secondly, I know not what *anything* is *in itself*, whether it be named of matter, or whether it be named of mind; and so matter as matter is not established, and mind as mind is not destroyed. Thirdly, there is no doubt but that the system— all that we know—the whole world—does lie, not indeed in the hollow of an Arab boy's hand, but in consciousness: all that we know are but modes of consciousness—bundles of our own consciousnesses. In this way, while there is a most pleasing *definiteness* for our *knowledge*, there is also a most pleasing *indefiniteness*, for our *ignorance*. Or in this way, while, in *knowledge*, science is secured its rights, and thought its freedom, we may quite satisfactorily limn God, free will, immortality, and all that sort of thing (if we really do want it) in the mist of our ignorance!

This is Mr Huxley's relative position—even to the irony, though that is not so certain. It is just possible in that respect, namely, that Mr Huxley is as simple and serious on the one side, as he is simple and serious on the other—as simple and serious and self-complacent in regard to ignorance, as he is simple, serious, and self-complacent in regard to knowledge. For my part, indeed, I must confess myself to find Mr Huxley, however valuable in his knowledge, much more interesting in his ignorance—in his ignorance and in the faith that is born of it. I don't know anything about *cause*, he seems to say to himself, or *substance*, or *actual externality;* and *therefore* there is all that —dream—possible! What a comfort, when the prose of know-

ledge wearies—when materialism is a horror to our natural
hopes—to possess in the poetry of ignorance a secret and sacred
chamber in which I can shut myself up legitimately to dream!
What a comfort to be able to retire to this *my* Fetish and strong
god to listen to my prayers! "Where ignorance is bliss, 'twere
folly to be wise;" and surely it is ignorance that is the blissful
side here. Sufficiently curious, it is, too, that the Revulsion, to
which *knowledge* is professedly all in all, cannot do, nevertheless,
without the refuge of ignorance. How Mr Buckle mouths
solemnly roundabout, in that ample, empty, pretentious way of
his, dwelling ever on the sacredness of a man's religious conviction, *which is for silence and secrecy alone!* One would think
it more natural that we should thank a man for *communicating*
to us that which, as most precious for him, might prove most
precious for us too. But no! gabble, chatter as you like about
your lower interests, but be absolutely silent about your higher
ones! That is the wisdom of the perfectly admirable Mr Buckle;
and Mr Huxley, as we see, is not without a certain approach to
it. Let us listen benevolently, he seems to say, to knowledge
in public; but let us all the more worship ignorance in private!
It is this ignorance we shall now consider in the order of its
three forms already named.

1. What concerns *causality* may be stated thus:—The material phenomena which constitute knowledge, are commonly
regarded as in *connection* the one with the other; but into the
nature of this connection, into the *necessity* of this connection,
we do not at all see. All that we do see is the *fact* of *invariable
association* among them. We certainly have grounds for the
expectation that this association *will* not vary; but these
grounds reducing themselves to this, that on the whole, it has
not yet varied; it is impossible for us to say, it *can* not, or it
must not vary. Knowing the fact only, and not its conditioning
reason, we are obliged to say in fairness, it *may* vary. When
the sun rises, it is day *this* day, and any day we ever heard of;
but to-morrow it may be night. A stone flung into the air
returns to-day, but to-morrow it may not. Cork floats at
present, but in the future it may sink. The knife cuts the
apple now, but an hour hence the apple may cut the knife.
To-day sugar sweetens tea, to-morrow it may salt it. To-day
the stick breaks the window, to-morrow the window may break
the stick. To-day the gunpowder but *repeats* the spark, to-
morrow it may *quench* it. To-day the cloak *de*pends, to-morrow
it may *sus*pend, etc., etc. Of course, we have no reason to expect
these changes; but we have no guarantee against them. We
do not any day know what "pastures new" await us. And
this is good; for this is philosophy, and in such philosophy we
have a checkmate to superstition, we have a checkmate to the

priest, who dare not any longer, in the face of such verifications, *dogmatise*.

2. These are great advantages, but they are not greater than those the same "New Philosophy" extends to us from the consideration of *substance*. What do I know about this that you call substance? Where is it? What is it? Can you let me see it? I will believe it when I see it. Meantime I know qualities only—I know all things in their qualities, not *in themselves*, not in their *substance*. And this, that we know not substance, is "the greatest discovery of psychology." Consider, too, how, in turn, it is related to infallible knowledge and—dogmas! We are emancipated from the priest when we can show him that we know appearances only. To pretend to know all *that*, when he does not know what bread is!

3. But a due application of the same principles to the question of *externality*, elicits even greater advantages perhaps, and in a double kind. For it not only secures us from what the priest can do *against* us, but it renders us independent of what he can do *for* us. I know no external world—namely, or I know no certainty of an external world. That fire that burns, that sea that rages—I know nothing of either but as a state of my own. What I know of external things—what I *can* know of external things *must* be in my consciousness. What are called such external things, then, are but bundles of my own consciousnesses. To tell me, consequently, all that miraculous story, is to tell me something which, even the existence of the external world being unguaranteed, I must hold also to be unguaranteed. This, at the same time, too, that my ignorance of any actual external world and of any necessity, whether of causality or substantiality in it, plenarily empowers imagination to bring to my feet, in freedom, all the good things the priest can only bring me in bondage—God, Immortality, Free-will.

This, then, is the "New Philosophy;" and who will deny its might, and its majesty? Knowledge is precipitation into a "slough," but ignorance is "escape!" To be awake with the understanding is to fall into "crass materialism;" but to dream with the imagination is to be safe within the crystal battlements of eternal idealism! Knowledge is but the wretched old oil-lamp, that spills, and bothers us with its wick and its filth; it is ignorance that is the Aladdin's lamp, and brings elysium!

But do these gentlemen mean it to be so? To Mr Bain, for example, is not the materialism all that is for him fundamental? and is not the idealism but, profanely to say it, the tongue in the cheek—to the priest, who incontinently sinks silent, dumbfounded? But how are *we* to look at this extraordinary *Zwitterling*, this extraordinary hermaphrodite? Is the world, then, no stable system of reason? Is it only as the unsteady iridescence in the water-drop in the Arab boy's hand? Thus and thus to-day, *may* all things work loose from one another to-morrow? Shall we never know anything but appearances—never know truth? Ah! well might Descartes doubt whether he who sent us were not "a powerful and malicious being who took pleasure in deluding us!"

But let us just see whether all these things cannot be looked at otherwise.

1. There is no *cause*, then; there is only a *first* followed by a *second*, an A by a B. Nexus between them there is none discernible: there is only one imagined. Under the name of *power*, it is familiar enough to conception to be sure, and current enough in speech, but, all the same, it is a mere fancy, a voluntary-involuntary phantasm, a gratuitous symbol, a vicarious image, a personified abstraction, a Comtian entity, an Hegelian Vorstellung—a myth!* The knowledge of this we owe to Hume, and this one point is the spore from which that vast bulk of German philosophy grew.

Nevertheless, it was but by counterstroke, so to speak, that from that spore this bulk grew; and it is not so certain that Hume's faith corresponded with his speech. Indeed, it is only a mistake, perhaps, to suppose that the sly Hume believed any such view of cause and effect, though, with his usual arch mischief, for perplexity to the priest, he wickedly started the difficulties that gave rise to it. Perfectly willing to "undermine the foundations" of anything whatever that had seemed hitherto only to serve "as a shelter to superstition," he knew all the same, that "Nature would always maintain her rights, and prevail in the end over any abstract reasoning whatsoever." So it was that, even when *just mentioning*—with such an air of simple reference to what was a matter of course for everybody—the *transparent fact*, that, "in all reasonings from experience, there is a step taken by the mind, which is not supported by any argument or process of the understanding"—so it was, I say,

* It is to this meaning I would confine the word *conception*, and for good and sufficient reasons, it may be, despite the *etymology*. *Idea* is, of course, *Idee*, and can take on every one of its significations. Kant, when exact and authoritative—Hegel always—translates *Begriff* by *Notio*. There is left only *Conception* for *Vorstellung*, and Hegel actually does render *Vorstellungen* by *Conceptionen*. *We have no choice then!* And reflection will only the more and more approve the result. *Representation*, for example, is a hideous word that will never pass current; and Dugald Stewart's admirable chapter on "Conception" will show that that word to him was quite the Hegelian Vorstellung. *Concept*, again, reminds too much of *conception* satisfactorily to render *Begriff*, and is, for the most part, only in philosophical use by an authority that in another generation will cease to be significant. All this, however, only where exactitude is required. Otherwise and in general, *idea* conveys perfectly well, not only *Begriff*, but even *Vorstellung*. *Any* interchange of the words in question is perhaps possible to the experienced translator, except only the unpardonable barbarism of *notion* for *Vorstellung*. *Notion* ought to be kept sacred for the *logical* notion.

that even when just mentioning this, and remarking that "we cannot penetrate into the reason of the conjunction" of cause and effect, he knew and admitted that that "step" and that "reason" lay in "a *natural* relation."

In reality, the whole thing has been, on the part of Hume, but a wicked riddle, the sly rogue (or the *arch* rogue if you will) always speaking with such an air of innocent conviction, that his allegation—"no reason can be discovered"—was taken at once without a moment's misgiving quite as the matter of fact for which it seemed to be taken by himself.

But, suppose we ask *now*—after all these years, and after all that breadth of clamour—*is* it matter of fact? Can it possibly be matter of fact? Must not the reason of the *conjunction* of things, as cause and effect, lie, as Hume admits, in "a *natural* relation?" And must not that natural relation be discoverable? In other words, must not "the step of the mind," the "process of the understanding," which Hume seemed to assume to fail, actually not fail? — and must it not be capable of being demonstrated?

Let the reader fully realise to himself what the assertion means, that the cause A is only an invariable *first*, and the effect B only an invariable *second*. All, so, is evidently reduced to the single character *succession*, and with the single predicate *invariable*, the explanation being added the *invariability* is only what we may call a *positive* one. That is: so far as we know yet, A *has* been first, B *has* been second, but this invariable succession so far as experience goes, must be seen to be what it is—only an invariable succession *so far as experience goes*. We have but a *fact* before us, we know not how, or whence, or why; we have absolutely no *reason* whatever *for* the fact. The succession *is*, *has* been, *may* be ; but it is a *dry* fact—a dry fact of *mere* succession. It is but a conjunction of *abstracts;* it is no *concrete* —no concrete of two, the one *from* the other, and *in* the other, and *through* the other. There is no *reason* in the very midst of the succession, by virtue of which the one is only because the other is. It is a fact that there is A *now*, and B *then;* there is no relation whatever between them but that of the order in time. A is A, B is B ; each on its own side is for itself, and *sui generis*, and independent. There is no community between them. They are absolutely disparate—heterogeneous. Each is foreign, alien to the other. Different from, they are indifferent to, each other. They are not inwardly in union; they are but outwardly beside each other. But for the order in time, they are not one whit more connected, the one with the other, than this ink-bottle and yonder coal-scuttle.

Surely the statement itself is its own involuntary *felo de se!* To the *humano capiti*, shall we join then the *cervicem equinam?*

Shall the *mulier formosa superne* be indeed desinent in the *atrum piscem?* Or if, whether for us, or the poet, there shall be a concrete that is rational, a concrete that is even *natural,* a concrete that *is* a concrete, shall not the one term, in all cases, *grow* out of the other? All will be different *then.* The terms shall not be heterogeneous, but homogeneous. The succession shall not be only *positively,* arbitrarily, invariable, but *necessarily, rationally* invariable. The succession, in fact, shall not be a succession at all. As what in *all* nature is closest, it shall be seen to be also what in its *own* nature is closest—not a succession, but a conjunction, a connection, a union, the most intimate, the most deeply inward union possible—at all events, the most intimate, the most deeply inward union the whole inorganic world can show.

Hume shall have simply hoaxed us, then—shall have simply hoaxed metaphysics — hoaxed metaphysics with his billiard balls, as Charles the Second did physics with his fish?

Yes; it is really so. Neither *à priori* nor *à posteriori* is there the incommunicable gulf in causality which Hume so naturally assumed, and so speciously glossed over.

Billiard balls are not by any means all that may be regarded, or alone what may be regarded, as types of causality. Here is a full sponge, and here is a hand that contracts on it—with an effect that is known. Have we here but an indifferent A, and an indifferent B, that are only outwardly beside each other, and not at all inwardly, and with reason, wrought together? Can we conceive of what happens here as but *succession*—a succession that, though thus to-day, may be otherwise to-morrow? A bit of wood weighed after immersion in water is found to be heavier than it was before immersion. In the same way, a letter that in India weighed under the ounce, may in England weigh over it. But, in either case, is the one fact but an indifferent *second* to the other? Expose the boards of a book to the fire, and, *Scotice,* they "*gizzen,*" but not without a perfect intelligence on our part of why. When the pound in the one scale plumps on the board, and the ounce in the other kicks the beam, does any one settle his chin in his neckerchief, and gravely expatiate on a first and a second in all times past that *may,* nevertheless, reverse themselves to-morrow? Surely arithmetic here has absolute possession—and to the perfect conviction of everybody —of the entire mystery! When to divide a sheet of paper evenly, I fold it in two and tear in the line of the fold, is the result a mere invariable consequent without perception of a reason? So, also, that a blunt knife is a better paper-cutter than a sharp one—surely we see why! Place a cannon ball on a sofa cushion, is the indentation that follows, a mere consequent, the reason of which we cannot understand. Doors

E

slam, shutters rattle, draughts whistle—in such events, or in the
action of windmills and watermills, of the teeth of saws or of
the teeth of men, can it be pretended that we have before us
only dry facts, the one now and the other again, but without
any reason of connection inwardly that makes the one but a
birth out of the other? Is it really just once for all so, that the
lees sink and the scum rises, or is there an explanation for both
events? When, overhearing your wonder at the strangely
blazing windows in a wood in France, the kindly Commère
threw in, "C'est par rapport au soleil, Messieurs!" was not that
rapport precisely the "step" the "understanding" wanted?
The Nile periodically overflows, but it does not only *just do so*
—we now know why. An eclipse involves, not only an invariable first, and an invariable second, but a reason as well.
It is surely not inexplicable why bodies throw shadows. So it
is also with day and night, with the seasons, with the tides—in
all these cases we have not only an invariable succession, but a
reasoned invariable succession. It is really no mystery why the
key fits the lock, or why Bruce's calthrops overthrew the
English horse. To varnish an egg preserves it, but we are not
left with the naked fact only, we can give an account of it as
well. If you turn a turtle on its back, you do not wonder at it
remaining so, any more than at the cut stalk falling, or the bladder
you prick collapsing. You do not draw your boots on with a
pair of skewers, and you do not say the only reason *why not* is
that boot-hooks are the invariable antecedents. Candle-making
(-dipping) admits of explanation. A glass-house is not the unconnected, the *dry* antecedent of strawberries at Christmas.
The navvie that digs, uses his pick first and his shovel second
—with perfect satisfaction as well to understanding as to perception. The paint on my house-door has its sufficient reason in
that painter's pot. Antarctic regions have more sea than Arctic
ones; and yet, though warmer in summer, they are colder in
winter; not without "*rapport*," perhaps, to the relative distance
at these seasons of the sun from either. The mason uses a
mallet of wood rather than a hammer of iron, and there is a
rationale of his act which is not uninteresting (in the case of
the mallet a deflection in striking hardly *tells*, and the action of
the point of the chisel is more delicately modifiable perhaps.)
The water that runs clear from the filter was brown when it
entered; but it has left its sufficient reason behind it. A wedge
splits a tree—this you understand, and you are not surprised
that a knife does not. The same breath that cools your soup
will warm your hands; but in neither case is the first to the
second only a *dry* one; it brings foison with it, and the virtue
that connects them. Why rag is better for a cut than paper,
why a watch-spring acts, why a stone hurts and a feather-

pillow does not—all that you see. The fire that hardens clay will soften wax: you can tell why in the one case, if, perhaps, not in the other. For this, too, is to be admitted, that we cannot always tell why. This, however, is but a moment's jar, *and the jar itself is the proof of the position.* . When the king, of the dumpling in Peter Pindar, wonders "How, how the devil got the apple in!" we laugh; but the wonder we laugh at is the *naive* confutation, as at hands of general mankind indeed, of the mere pedantry that has made Hume's riddle a *theory!* If *here* got *there*, there must have been a *door of communication* between them. In all cases of causality, the first is not just on this side and the other just on that side, because it is once for all just so: in all cases of causality there is—whether we know it or not— a *door of communication* between the two sides. Hume made believe to shut this door up, and half a dozen worthy men have taken him at his word!

It is worth while considering, however, that the very men who—*explicitly*—deny all this sort of concrete virtue in the facts themselves, and assert as well a mere provisional invariability as a mere dry succession of an abstract first and an abstract second—those very men are in certain circumstances very interestingly forward to refute themselves—*implicitly*. Just tell Mr Mill that Moses with a dry rod brought water from a dry rock! I do not think that that eminent philosopher will have any difficulty *there*. And yet if causality is but a *succession*—a succession that *may* vary—a succession in which the first is *only* the first, the second *only* the second—one would expect, on the part of Comte and his disciples, rather a desire to accept the miracle than that hot haste to reject it. Nay, the miracle they refuse at the hands of Moses, they are ready to accept at the hands of Mr Crosse: they are quite ready to believe it possible for *him* to grind *wet* maggots out of *dry* electricity!

It may illustrate the position, at all events, should I say here that the impossibility the Revulsion feels in regard to miracles is precisely the impossibility I feel in regard to abstract succession. I cannot entertain the idea of mere *positivity* of association, without community, without intermediating nexus. Very curious! Our modern Berkeleians, too, wry themselves into the same *in*humanity: they, too, see indifferent units indifferently in succession, but at the will of God—contriving to secure for themselves thus (see Browning's "Caliban") a Setebos to worship, and the creation of a Setebos to admire!

Independent succession is no belief of society at large, however, in which reference I hold Sir John Herschel to name the true concrete state of the case (in his "Astronomy," p. 232), thus :—

"Whatever attempts have been made by metaphysical

writers to reason away the connection of cause and effect, and fritter it down into the unsatisfactory relation of habitual sequence, it is certain that the conception of some more real and intimate connection is quite as strongly impressed upon the human mind as that of the existence of an external world."

Beyond all doubt, then, there is a certain community between the cause and the effect, and in this community lies the reason of the nexus. In short, the reason of the causal nexus is—Identity. "The rain," says Hegel, "is the cause of the wetness," "but it is the same water in the wetness that is in the rain." It is the same physical water on the street, then, that was in the cloud, and, similarly, the water in my beard is the same physical water that was in my breath. A like state of the case is visible in every one of the various examples of causality that we have seen above.

Nor is it different with Hume's billiard balls : it is identically the same motion now in the one that was then in the other, and the examination of *them*, before the motion, or after the motion, as *independent individuals*, was beside the point. That is, abstraction was made by Hume from all that constituted causality in the balls, and no wonder he could not find in them what he himself had just thrown out. The motion was alone the cause, and it was idle to examine *them* apart from *it*. And here we see that what are regarded as causes are, commonly, concrete objects with a variety of elements in them beside that or those which may stand at the moment in the causal nexus. *Contraction* in the hand, and in the sponge; *water* in the cloud, and on the street; *motion* in the bat, and in the ball : in all such cases we see but a single *import*, and it is *common* to the cause and to the effect. It, in effect, is *both*. So far as this *import* goes, then, there is a relation of identity between the cause and the effect, however different *they* are otherwise. They are not only *externally associated*, they are *internally united*—they are united in a relation of identity, and this, whatever elements of difference they may bring with them otherwise. The hand is very different from the sponge, the cloud from the street, the ball from the bat ; but as copula between the respective pairs of *differents*, we have, in order, the identity of contraction, of water, and of motion. The knife cuts the apple : shall we, like Hume, examine knife and apple apart, and say how *different* they are—blinding ourselves to the one single absolute identity that is in the cause and the effect of which they are but the vehicles ?

Sometimes, too, plainly, the identity may not be *explicit*, but only *implicit*; or it may even be present in the form of diversity. It is really by identity that you would explain shadows, eclipses, etc., and yet the shadow (darkness) is the reverse of light.

This, then, is the assertion : In all cases of causality, the tie, the copula, denied by Hume really exists; the "step taken by the mind" really *is* supported on a " process of the understanding;" this tie, copula, step, process, has—explicitly, or implicitly—its grounds and sufficient reason in Identity.

One can conjecture much opposition here. Is the pain of a burn identical with the flame that caused it, then ? This, one can hear the Revulsion bawl out ; to a man ! Causality as such, however, ceases with the inorganic world. *As such*, it has no place in will, reason ; and vitality itself has already set bounds to it —not but that a good stick may smash·my skull and my wife's pipkin on precisely the same principles.

It is the motion, then, that is both the true cause and the true effect in the case of the billiard balls. In the ordinary row of such balls suspended for experiment by strings, the motion with which the last leaps off is precisely the same motion with which the first was allowed to impinge. It may seem a contradiction and a difficulty here that *both* balls—the first and the last— being allowed, at once, and similarly, to impinge on the rest, the one motion seems merely to be counteracted and destroyed by the other. Is the *double* motion, thus, then, only neutralised and lost ? No; the motion counterbalanced in mass reappears in molecule; and we meet here the doctrine of the Conserva- tion of Force or Energy. Not quite stable in its metaphysics yet, this doctrine is probably sound, so far, in its physics. Light and heat, however they may express themselves to sentiency, or to a medium that *dilates* on molecular *vibration*, are, *in themselves*, it seems, only motions, as magnetism, galvanism, etc., in some unexplained way, may also be. In that case, we may conceive nothing in space but matter and motion. Nay, in that case, may we not *conceive* nothing in space but motion alone ? Matter itself shall be but counterbalanced motion—as it were *implicit* motion, which the flutter of a feather, in changing the direction of opposing tendencies, may instantly render *explicit*. A weight on a spring—these are but counter- vailing motions, and the slightest shift would enable them to express themselves. The earth itself, then, may be conceived —not that I deny matter—as but a congeries of belts of countervailing motions; and something of a rational basis may be seen thus to be extended to those who *feign* matter to be the expression of innumerable centres—whence, what, or how, one knows not !—of force. The fact of *countervailing* motion must be allowed, however, to demonstrate — as in the spring and the weight—the reality of motion without its expression. One can see also the possible *dispersion* of any

motion in mass through the conduction of motion in molecule
—vibration.*

It is through this doctrine of the conservation of force that,
in regard to causality, Mr Bain, with a very proper air of
modest self-denial, makes a clutch at originality. He attributes
to himself the "innovation" of "rendering" "cause" "by the
new doctrine called the Conservation of Force," etc. But is
such "clutch" possible to one who denies *power*, and asserts
succession only? There is the mechanical equivalent of heat:
what meaning can M E have for Mr Bain? Will he believe
that there is heat *here*, and M E *there*, only as two units of a
mere succession which in their own nature are not identical?
Manifestly, there is a *community of nature* in the two sides of
the conservation of force that summarily truncates any use of
them by Mr Bain—at the same time that it is admirably
corroborative of the true theory of causality which places its
principle in Identity. Heat is motion, and really precisely the
same motion is M E. When stopped by a wall (say), the motion
of a cannon ball vanishes as in mass, but reappears as in
molecule—heat. We see, then, in such an example, very
strikingly, how the virtue that conjoins the two terms in
causality is Identity. *Power*, therefore, is no abstraction, but has
an *implement*, a *filling*—of *identity*. Instead, consequently, of the
conservation of force explaining causality, as is preposterously
the proposition of Mr Bain, it is causality that, on the contrary,
explains *it*. That is, Causality, as the universal, subsumes the
Conservation of Force, as the particular, under it. It is but
inconsistency, then, in Mr Bain, that—though the *temptation*
may be acknowledged—would lead him, self-paralysed, as he is,
in regard to *power*, to the *clutch* alluded to.

With reference to Mr Huxley, now, the result, so far, is
this:—There *is* a necessary nexus in the relation of cause and
effect, and no interest of spirit is to be rescued from materialism by the denial of it.

2. Nor is this one whit more possible by means of the
expedient that we do not know things *in themselves*—that we
only know phenomena—that we do not know what *substance*
is. Mr Huxley's reason for ignorance here is precisely my
reason, and everybody else's, for knowledge. As little as the
causal nexus disappears because it is no mere affair of sense,
so little does substance disappear for any similar reason. We

---

* It is not in any man's power, then, to set bounds to the *stored motion* of the
universe, and it is not even in any man's power to prove the molecular motion of the
sun perishable. If all energy *must* end, why *has it not* ended? The infinitude of the
past gives the same possibility of an end in the past, as the infinitude of the future
the possibility of an end in the future. Energy, then, has either begun, or has always
been. If *begun*, the principles of the beginning, in all probability, *still are;* if *always
been*, then it *always will be.*

can know a substance only through its qualities, and it is but
an absurdity to adduce this, our knowledge of it, only as the
proof and the guarantee of our ignorance of it. Consider this!
We know substance only by reason of qualities, therefore we
do *not* know it. That is, we do *not* know by means of the very
reason through which we *do* know! Is not this a mere paying
of ourselves with words? A thing that does not act can
never be known, and is only equal to nothing. Is it reasonable, then, to say that, precisely when it makes itself known by
acting, precisely then it makes itself unknown by acting, as if
it had never acted? How else *can* a thing be known but by
acting—by its qualities? and is the only medium of admission
to be made also the single medium of exclusion! We do not
know things in themselves, because we only know what they
are for us! Well, but what they are *for us*, is really what
they are *in themselves*? A thing, a substance, is not a bundle,
is not a *collection* of qualities; it is as much an intussusception
of its qualities as an ego is of its ideas. There is not greenness
here in this crystal, transparency there, and sourness yonder.
It is the substance, the single and individual unit, the *it*, that is
green, and likewise transparent, and also sour. Would you
have me, in independence of the greenness, and transparency,
and sourness, take you out the *it*, and show it you? and even
then, would you be able to *know* it, but as otherwise or similarly
green, and transparent, and sour, etc. If you will blindfold yourself
then you *must*; but it is your own act. I know the character of a
man only by knowing what this character is for me; but do I not
also then know what it is in itself? After I have thoroughly
put myself at home with Shakespeare, or Burns, or Cromwell,
am I immediately to turn round and stultify myself by figure-
ing some substance, some *in itself* that is only gratuitous and
foreign to the case. Mr Huxley is in his chamber: Does he
then mystify himself into an impossible chaos by muttering to
himself—Ah, that fire, that carpet, that table, these chairs, these
books, they are really something quite else than what they are
for me—what they are for me is a small matter—nothing—but
what they are *not* for me—Ah! that *were* something, did I but
know that! Does Mr Huxley really hide from himself what
that picture on the wall is for him and in itself, by disconsolately
murmuring, I am absolutely ignorant—I can never know what
canvas, what hemp is in itself? Is not all that talk about an
in itself that is not for him idle? Does he not *inhabit* the room?
and is it not a thoroughly-intelligible system? So with the
world: it is an intelligible—external—system. This stone
that I take up, am I really to mystify or stultify myself in its
regard by saying—If my muscles were infinitely stronger, it
would dissolve in my grasp? It *is* black, it *might* be red.

What then? Is not the lobster boiled the same lobster that it was unboiled? Mr Huxley, surely, does not expect us to follow him into that silly, wholly antiquated and effete rubbish that bids us cross our fingers to examine a pea, or squint our eyes to look at the table. Shall we, then, only behold the world aright—by putting our head between our legs? Is a cramp truth, convulsions reason, or distortion philosophy?

I do know substance, and I know it by and through the qualities with which I know so well how to serve myself. Here is a printed Shakespeare: is there in its regard an *in itself* which I do not know, but which, if known, would dwarf into insignificance all that I do know? Why, I do know it in itself —its very paper and boards, if you like—I know them in themselves too. There is no such thing anywhere in it as this in itself, that is said to be unknown. All that the book need be, should be, can be—in itself, it is for me. The true *in itself* there is Shakespeare's soul, and that I have access to—at least, all that *can* be done *is* done for my access. Thinkers like Mr Huxley are very wroth at *obscurantism;* but, by the same involuntary retribution through which they fall into the miraculous by fleeing it, they themselves are the obscurantists proper. At the very moment that they insist on knowledge, they insist also on dream—a dream that stultifies all knowledge into fragments of an unknown inane. We must not delude ourselves with phrases, then—phrases that are but subterfuges and evasions. God has not sent us to know only mockeries here—appearances. On the contrary, He has given it us to know things— things in themselves—a concrete *system* of things, as well external as internal, that is perfectly intelligible.

3. And this brings us to Mr Huxley's last ignorance—the ignorance of *externality,* the reason for which is that we know only consciousnesses, and *in* consciousness. Mr Huxley makes only a convenience of this, however; in his actual world it is no ingredient. That actual world is simply materialism; and the idealism it talks of in consciousness is only, as it were, an occasional flash from a private lantern that is peculiarly convenient at times for the reassurance of others, perhaps of ourselves! Let us have the materialism of knowledge for our daily work, he says, but the idealism of ignorance for our nightly dream—and the good of our souls, if we will! The expedient, therefore, does not seem a very hopeful one—an expedient that would counsel reason to take refuge in ignorance. But neither are the facts on its side. That we only know *within* is no reason that what we know may not be really *without.* The truth is that we can test it, and try it, and lay stumbling blocks in the way of it, and experiment on it, and prove it in a thousand ways—to the result that we do know an actually independent

external system of things. To attempt to crush all this into the water-drop in the hollow of an Arab boy's hand, or, what is about the same thing, into the point of consciousness, and *leave* it there, is but supererogatory delusion, and the trick of a word.

But, so, we have a demonstration at once of the nullity of Mr Huxley's "extrication" and of the reality of his materialism. Doubt is always an unusual substitute for certainty ; but doubt in regard to causality, or substantiality, or externality, is gratuitous and unfounded. We must decline, then, the safe-guard of scepticism with which Mr Huxley would make believe to protect us from materialism ; and even hint, but as gently as possible, that he who, at the hour that now is, would seriously proffer us—(the two fingers gravely crossed over the pea !)—any such doctrines, is, philosophically, as late, as he was, physiologically, precipitate. Perhaps that he is late in the one case is the why he was precipitate in the other. But, all that being so, at the same time that he would express all phenomena in terms of matter—would explain mind itself by the "disposi-tion of mere material molecules," I cannot see that Mr Huxley is possessed of any—the very smallest—reason for refusing for himself the name of materialist. When he has placed *materialism* as an entire *system* of *knowledge* over or on his right hand, he cannot expect much confidence from us in what *may* be the sneer that points to *ignorance*, and the *word* idealism, profanely to say it, *over the left*. Would Mr Huxley but really take refuge in the principle of Descartes—self-consciousness ! Is philosophy —are the philosophers, Plato, Aristotle, Plotinus, Proclus, Descartes, Spinosa, Locke, Leibnitz, Berkeley, Hume, Kant, Hegel—these, and all the rest, with their enormous writings—are they only there to say, We know nothing but successive phenomena *in* consciousness ? Knowing that, are we dispensed from the *labour* of the region ? Knowing that, and saying that, are we, while we work only *for* science, and *in* matter, perfectly cultivated, enlightened minds in the centre who hold the balance even ? That is in one word the position of Mr Huxley ; but is it likely that the vast, heaven-scaling mountain of philosophy has yielded only such a drowned mouse of a result ? And can we claim to be philosophers by knowing no more ? It is quite certain, however, that Messrs Mill and Bain write enormous books and for no other result—After all, then, Mr Huxley may have his own excuse ! It is for us to know, nevertheless, that the position is wrong—that philosophy, perhaps, only begins where Mr Huxley ends ; for the problem of said phenomena is to it—*what* they are, not simply *that* they are. But into this, plainly, we cannot enter at present.

NOTE.

It is argued by Mr Huxley in his essay on "Yeast," as against Kant, who conceived generally, "the special peculiarity of the living body to be that the parts exist for the sake of the whole, and the whole for the sake of the parts," that by the resolution of the living body "into an aggregation of quasi-independent cells," "this conception has ceased to be tenable." But it is not so certain that this is so, whether as regards the cells, or as regards the body. A cell is still a *whole* of *parts*, and both parts and whole are in the relation assigned by Kant. Then, when the actual inter-connections of the body and the cells are studied, the result is not what Mr Huxley would seem to infer as to the *primacy*, so to speak, and independence of the cells. They, rather, are seen to be but subservient ministers, while the body itself is the prime and dominating agent. In illustration here, let me quote from my review of Dr Beale's recent work on Protoplasm, in the *Edinburgh Courant* for February 25, 1870 :—

" All the tissues and organs of which we consist are built up, according to Dr Beale, by millions of minute living particles. Each of these is a unit of *germinal matter*, surrounded or faced by *formed material*. This formed material goes to constitute the tissue or organ—skin, muscle, bone, liver, lung, etc.—in which the living particle of germinal matter finds itself . . . Materials from the blood constantly pass into the centres of the particles of the germinal matter. These particles are thus fed, for they convert the materials they receive into their own substance, at the same time that, at their own surfaces, they themselves are constantly passing into the non-living state of formed material. This, then, is the process. *Germinal matter* (a cell) converts *pabulum* (from the blood) into itself, multiplies, and lastly dies (in an external ring or external surface) into formed material. The three matters italicised constitute thus Dr Beale's physiological elements, and of these the germinal matter alone lives. . . . The least erudite reader may be able to form to himself, perhaps now, a perfectly clear idea of the nature, place, and business of these working units (the cells or germinal particles) in the general economy. It is not difficult for any one to picture a skeleton, or to conceive it filled up with muscles, and covered with skin. As little difficult will it be, imaginatively, to place lungs, heart, stomach, and viscera, within the trunk, and to connect every part of these, as well as of bone, muscle, and skin, with the marrowy brain within the skull, by means of the threads of the nerves. These are the general outlines of the structure, and this structure is now on the whole to be conceived as *formed material* thrown up by millions of germinal particles seated beneath or around it. The entire surface of the skin, for example, is to be conceived as so much formed material casing so many millions of germinal particles that cluster over its inner surface. Vessels, again, in similar illustration, are to be viewed as so many pipes and pipelets, the solid canals of which are only the formed material of innumerable germinal particles around them. In this way, then, the germinal particles almost show as so many living *paving-beetles* constantly pushing *up* the continuity of the streets and walls—of the bone, skin, brain, that constitute man. But this being so, is it possible to avoid realising to ourselves, and in a very vivid manner, the absurdity of the pretensions of Mr Huxley to materialise all the processes of the organism by means of the microscope? Why, of this organisation itself as such—that is, of the mechanical apparatus it presents to us—the microscope tells us nothing whatever. The microscope only enables us to see a single *paving-beetle*, a single cell, a single germinal particle in connection with more or less of its own portion of formed material—a single coral, so to speak, and the polype that died into it : it tells us nothing whatever of the vast machine which these polypes have all unconsciously built up with their coral. The mighty and complex fabric of man is, after all, despite its innumerable parts, a unity : all these parts but go towards that unity, are sublated into it. Now, what of all that does microscopic observation tell us? Why, simply nothing. Myriads of miserable Egyptians carried stones to the Pyramid ; but no microscopic watching of any one of these, stone and all, would ever explain the Pyramid itself—*its* many to a one. So with the frame of man; on which, would we understand it aright, it is infinitely more necessary to turn the lens, so to speak, of an all-embracing telescope, than to turn on its infinitesimal particles the minuteness of the microscope. . . . It must be evident, indeed, that the microscopic particle throws but small light on, so to speak, the telescopic whole. Consider the supply of pabulum alone. If with that pabulum the germinal particles build up individually the various units of the machine, it is the machine itself, and as a whole, that supplies that pabulum. Nay, it is the machine itself that properly alone lives, that connects all particles, living or dead, into a unity and purpose of which unity the particles themselves, whether living or dead, know naught. . . . The probability is, then, that the germinal particles have little action besides providing for the keeping up of the tissues, and that it is on these tissues, for the most part, that the functions of the single unity depend."

In short, man's life is in his mechanism as a whole—in his coral; and not in the polypes that supplied it to him. That is, it is the so-called dead formed material that alone truly lives, and not the so-called living germinal matter that is assumed to die into it. Or, as I said at first, the cells are but as servants to the body itself, which is alone the lord; the primacy lies with the latter and not with the former; Kant's dictum is as valid to-day as it was yesterday.